## "Maybe you could find your razor. You're badly in need of a shave."

She hesitated, then continued, "I could do it for you, if you like. My brother broke two fingers on his right hand once and I—"

"No. Let me do it by myself."

She went to change the sheets and returned to the bathroom to find him still sitting at the sink. There were uneven patches of beard on his cheeks and a trickle of blood down his chin. Wordlessly, he handed the razor to her, grimaced and squeezed his eyes shut.

She'd thought that shaving Freeman would be no different than shaving her brothers, but as she stood there looking at him, she realized it was.

Her pulse quickened, and she felt a warm flush beneath her skin. Shaving Freeman was more intimate than she'd supposed it would be and she was thankful that his dark eyes were closed.

"All done."

"Thank you."

"You look a lot better." And he did, more than better. He had the kind of good looks that cautious mothers warned their daughters against.

**Emma Miller** lives quietly in her old farmhouse in rural Delaware. Fortunate enough to be born into a family of strong faith, she grew up on a dairy farm, surrounded by loving parents, siblings, grandparents, aunts, uncles and cousins. Emma was educated in local schools and once taught in an Amish schoolhouse. When she's not caring for her large family, reading and writing are her favorite pastimes.

### Books by Emma Miller

### Love Inspired

### *The Amish Matchmaker*

*A Match for Addy*
*A Husband for Mari*
*A Beau for Katie*

### *Lancaster Courtships*

*The Amish Bride*

### *Hannah's Daughters*

*Courting Ruth*
*Miriam's Heart*
*Anna's Gift*
*Leah's Choice*
*Redeeming Grace*
*Johanna's Bridegroom*
*Rebecca's Christmas Gift*
*Hannah's Courtship*

Visit the Author Profile page at Harlequin.com for more titles.

# A Beau for Katie

## Emma Miller

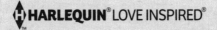

**H HARLEQUIN**® LOVE INSPIRED®

Recycling programs
for this product may
not exist in your area.

LOVE INSPIRED BOOKS

ISBN-13: 978-0-373-81924-9

A Beau for Katie

Copyright © 2016 by Emma Miller

www.Harlequin.com

**Printed in U.S.A.**

He who finds a wife finds what is good
and receives favor from the Lord.
—*Proverbs* 18:22

# *Chapter One*

❧

*Millside Amish Community,*
*Kent County, Delaware*
*July*

Suddenly apprehensive, Katie Byler reined in her horse on the bridge, easing the buggy to a standstill. Next to the dam was the feed-and-grain mill, a business that had been there since colonial times and was one of the few water-powered mills left in Delaware. On the far side was the millpond, a large stretch of water surrounded for the most part by trees. Out in the middle of the pond, a pair of Canada geese bobbed, and overhead, iridescent dragonflies and some sort of birds swooped and fluttered. It was a beautiful sight with the morning light sparkling on the blue-green water, and on any other day, Katie would have taken delight in it. Today, however, she had serious concerns on her mind.

She may have let Sara Yoder talk her into something she'd regret.

Behind her, Sara, the county's only Amish matchmaker, stopped her mule and climbed down from her buggy. "What's wrong?" She came to stand beside Katie's cart. "Why did you stop?" Sara raised her voice to be heard above the rush of water under the bridge. "We're blocking traffic."

Katie made a show of looking in both directions, up and down the road. It was a private lane, and anyone using it would be coming to or leaving the mill. At the moment, the parking lot in front of the mill had only one car and it was parked, with no one inside. The lane behind her was empty. "*Ne*, I don't think so," she answered in Deitsch, the German dialect that the Amish used among themselves.

"Don't tell me you're having second thoughts." Sara folded her arms over her bosom and gave Katie *the look* from beneath her black bonnet, the look that had given Sara a reputation for taking no nonsense. "You said you would accept the job, and I gave Jehu my word that you would start this morning."

"I know I agreed to it, but now…" She met Sara's strong-minded attitude with her own.

She liked the middle-aged woman, admired her really. Sara had gumption. She was an independent woman in a traditional society where most widows depended on fathers or sons to provide for them.

Katie narrowed her gaze on the matchmaker. Sara didn't have the pale Germanic skin of most Amish; she was half African American, with a coffee-colored complexion and dark, textured hair. Katie knew Sara's heritage because she'd asked her the first time they'd met. "How do I know that you're not trying to match me with Freeman Kemp?" she asked. "Because if you are, I'll tell you right off, it's a hopeless cause. He's one man I'd never consider for a husband."

Katie and Freeman had clashed when they were volunteering as helpers at a wedding the previous November. She'd been in charge of one of the work parties, and she'd made a suggestion about the way the men were loading chairs into the church wagon. Freeman had taken affront and had behaved immaturely, stalking off to sulk while the other men continued to work. It hadn't been an argument exactly, but it was clear that although her way was far more sensible, Freeman was offended by being told what to do by a woman. Katie couldn't have cared less. Growing up with older brothers, she'd learned early to speak up for herself, and if Freeman disliked her because of her refusal to be submissive, that was his problem.

Sara arched one dark brow and sighed. "Poor Freeman is laid up in bed with a broken femur. He hasn't asked me to find him a wife, and if he *did* discover he needed one this week, I doubt you're in any danger of him running you down and dragging you before the bishop." She shrugged. "It's because of his injury that he needs a housekeeper. You have no need for concern about your reputation, if that's your worry. Freeman's grandmother lives right next to him in the little house. She's in and out of Freeman's place all day long, and she'll provide the chaperoning the elders expect."

"That's not what worries me," Katie muttered. Sara was just like her: she never minced words. "I just don't want any misunderstandings. Freeman Kemp is one of those men all the single girls moon over. You know, him being so good-looking and so well-to-do." She nodded in the direction of the mill and surrounding property, the farmhouse and little *grossmama haus* where his grandmother lived. "I wouldn't want him to think that I'm one of them."

Sara laid a small brown hand on the dashboard of Katie's buggy. "If you're intimidated by Freeman, I'm sure I can get someone else to take the job. I wouldn't want to force you to do anything that made you feel uncomfortable."

"I'm not *intimidated* by him." Katie sat up a little straighter, tightened the reins in her hands and gazed ahead at the farmhouse. "Certainly not." She was probably making too much of a small incident. Freeman *had* made a remark about her bossiness to a friend of her brother's not long after the wedding incident, but he'd probably forgotten all about the unpleasantness by now.

"Good." Sara patted Katie's knee. "Then there's no reason to keep them waiting any longer. The sooner you start, the sooner you can put the house in order."

"Well, Uncle Jehu, if you hired a housekeeper without my say-so, you can just *un-hire* her." Freeman lay propped up on pillows in a daybed against the kitchen wall. "We need a strange woman rattling around here about as much as I need another broken leg."

"Now, boy, calm yourself," the older man said quietly in Deitsch. His arthritis-gnarled fingers moved, twisting a cord in a continuous game of cat's cradle, forming one shape after another. "It's only temporary. A younger pair of willing hands might bring some order to this mess we call a house."

Freeman glanced away. His uncle meant no insult. Calling him *boy* was a term of affection, but Freeman felt it was demeaning sometimes. He was thirty-five years old and he'd been running the family mill since he was twenty. Everyone in their Amish community accepted him as a grown man and head of this house, but because he'd never married, his uncle still thought of him as a stripling.

Uncle Jehu gestured with his chin in the general direction of the kitchen sink where Freeman's grandmother stood washing their breakfast dishes. "No insult meant to you, Ivy."

Freeman's paternal grandmother bobbed her head in agreement. "None taken. I said from the start when I came to live here I wouldn't be anyone's housekeeper. I've plenty of chores to keep me busy at my own place, not to mention waiting on customers at the mill. And what with my arthritis, I can't do it all." She eyed her grandson, sitting up in the bed, his leg cast from ankle to upper thigh, resting in a cradle of homemade quilts. "Jehu's right, Freeman. This house can stand a good cleaning. There are more cobwebs in this kitchen than the hayloft."

"You think I don't see them?" Freeman swallowed his rising impatience and forced himself not to raise his voice. "As soon as I get this cast off, I'll *redd* it all up. I did fine before I broke my leg, didn't I?" He still felt like a fool, breaking his leg the way he did. Anyone who'd been raised around farm animals should have known to take care and get a friend to lend a hand. He'd just been too sure of himself, and his own pride had gotten the better of him.

Ivy shook a soapy finger at him. "Stop fussing and make the best of it." She dipped a coffee cup in rinse water and stacked it in the drainer. "Maybe the Lord put this hurdle in your path to make you take stock of your own shortcomings. You've a good heart. You're always eager to help others, but you've never had the grace to accept help when you need it." She drew her mouth into a tight purse and nodded. "Jehu's already arranged the girl's hire for two weeks."

"And she's coming this morning," his uncle said as he twisted the string into a particularly intricate pattern. "So accept it gracefully and make her welcome."

A motor vehicle horn beeped from the parking lot.

"Another customer," Grossmama declared, quickly drying her hands on a dishtowel. "We're going to have another busy one at the mill. Didn't I say that buying those muslin bags with *Kemp's* printed on them and advertising would pay off? The Englishers drive from all over the state to get our stone-ground bread flour." Retrieving her black bonnet from the table, she put it on over her prayer *kapp*, and bustled out the door.

"With a housekeeper, we might get something to eat other than oatmeal," Uncle Jehu offered his nephew by way of consolation.

"I heard that!" his grandmother called back through the screen door. "Nothing wrong with oatmeal. I eat it every day, and I've never been sick a day in my life."

"Never sick a day in her life," his uncle repeated under his breath.

Freeman couldn't help chuckling. He was as tired of oatmeal as Uncle Jehu. There was nothing wrong with his grandmother's oatmeal. It was tasty and filling, but after eating it every morning since he was discharged from the hospital, he longed for pork sausage, bacon, over-easy eggs and home fries. And he was tired of her chicken noodle soup that they ate for dinner and supper most days, unless a neighbor was kind enough to drop by with a meal. "A few more days and I'll be up and about," he told his uncle. "I can take over the cooking, like I used to."

His uncle scoffed. "Unless you want to end up back in the hospital, you'll follow doctor's orders. A broken thighbone's a serious thing. In the meantime, the house is getting away from us, and so is the laundry." He shook his head. "It's a good thing I'm blind. Otherwise I would have been ashamed to go to church in a shirt that's been worn three Sundays and not been washed and ironed."

"No. Housekeeper," Freeman repeated firmly, emphasizing each syllable.

Jehu's terrier, Tip, leaped off the bed and ran barking to the door.

"Too late." Uncle Jehu broke into a self-satisfied grin. "Sounds like a buggy coming. Must be Sara Yoder and her girl now."

"You should send her back. We don't need her," Freeman protested, but only half-heartedly. He knew the battle was lost. He wouldn't hurt the poor girl's feelings by sending her away now that she was here. He would have to make the best of it.

"*Ne.* You heard Ivy. I already hired her." Jehu didn't sound a bit repentant; in fact, he seemed quite pleased with himself.

Freeman had a lot of respect for his mother's oldest brother, and more than that, he loved him. It was a pity when a man couldn't be master in his own house. Freeman was used to having his grandmother living in the *grossmama haus.* She'd been part of the household even before his parents died, and the two of them got along as easily as chicken and dumplings.

But Uncle Jehu had only come to live with him the previous summer and didn't always seem to understand that Freeman liked to do things his own way. Caring for his uncle was his responsibility, and he was glad to do it, but he didn't want to have decisions made for him as if he were still a child.

"Fine," Freeman muttered, feeling frustrated that he couldn't even get up to greet Sara and the housekeeper properly. It was demeaning to be laid out in a bed like this. But after a complication the previous week, his surgeon had been adamant. Freeman needed to keep his leg elevated at all times for another three days. "Who is this housekeeper? Do I know her?"

"She's from Apple Valley church district, but the two of you have probably crossed paths somewhere."

"You can at least tell me her name if you're forcing me to have her in my house."

His uncle looked up, sightless brown eyes calm and peaceful. "Name's Katie. Katie Byler."

"Katie Byler!" Freeman repeated. "Absolutely not." He flinched as he spoke and pain shot up his leg. He groaned, reaching down to steady his casted leg. "Not Katie Byler, Uncle Jehu. Anyone but Katie Byler." He frowned. "She's the bossiest woman I ever met."

His uncle chuckled. "I thought you said your

*mudder* was the bossiest woman you ever met. *Ya,* I distinctly remember you saying that." He rose, tucked his loop of string into his trousers' pocket and made his way to the door. He chuckled again. "And maybe my sister was. But I never saw that it did your father any harm."

"Please, Uncle Jehu," Freeman groaned. "Get someone else. *Anybody* else."

"Too late," his uncle proclaimed. He pushed open the door and grinned. "Sara, Katie. Come on in. Freeman and I've been waiting for you."

Katie followed Sara into the Kemp house, pausing just inside the doorway to allow her vision to adjust to the interior after the bright July sunshine.

"Here's Katie," Sara announced, "just as I promised, Jehu. She'll lend a hand with the housework until he's back on his feet." She motioned Katie to approach the bed. "I think you two already know each other."

*"Ya,"* Freeman admitted gruffly. "We do."

"We're so glad you could come to help out," his uncle said. "As you can see by this mess, you haven't come a day too early."

Katie removed her black bonnet, straightened her spine, and took in a deep breath. The girls were right about one thing; Freeman Kemp wasn't hard on the eyes. Even lying flat in a bed, one leg encased in an uncomfortable-looking cast, he was still a striking figure of a man. The indoor pallor and the pain lines at the corners of his mouth couldn't hide the clean lines of his masculine jaw, his white, even teeth, or his straight, well-formed nose and forehead. His wavy brown hair badly needed a haircut, and he had at least a week's growth of dark beard, but the sleeveless cotton undershirt revealed a tanned neck, and broad, muscular shoulders and arms.

Freeman's compelling gaze met hers. His eyes were brown, not the walnut shade of Sara's but a golden brown, almost amber, with darker swirls of color, and they were framed in lashes far too long for a man.

Had he caught her staring at him? Unnerved, she recovered her composure and concealed her embarrassment with a solicitous smile. "Good morning, Freeman," she uttered in a hushed tone.

Puzzlement flickered behind Sara's inquisitive eyes, and then her apple cheeks crinkled in a sign of amused understanding. She moved closer to the bed, blocking Katie's view of Freeman's face and his of hers and began to pepper him with questions about his impending recovery.

Rescued, Katie turned away to inspect the

kitchen that would be her domain for the next two weeks. She'd never been inside the house before, just the mill, but from the outside, she'd thought it was beautiful. Now, standing in the spacious kitchen, she liked it even more. It was clear to her that this house had been home to many generations, and someone, probably a sensible woman, had carefully planned out the space. Modern gas appliances stood side by side with tidy built-in cabinets and a deep soapstone sink. There was a large farm table in the center of the room with benches on two sides, and Windsor chairs at either end. The kitchen had big windows that let in the light and a lovely old German open-shelved cupboard. The only thing that looked out of place was the bed containing the frowning Freeman Kemp.

"You must be in a lot of pain," Sara remarked, gently patting Freeman's cast.

"*Ne.* Nothing to speak of."

"He is," Jehu contradicted. "Just too stubborn to admit to it. He'll accept none of the pain pills the doctor prescribed."

Freeman's eyes narrowed. "They gave them to me at the hospital. I couldn't think straight."

Katie nodded. "You're wise to tough it out if you can. Too many people start taking those things and then find that they can't do without them. Rest and proper food for an invalid will do you the most good."

Freeman glanced away, as if feeling uncomfortable at being the center of attention. "I'm not an invalid."

Katie sighed, wondering if a broken femur had been the man's only injury or if he'd taken a blow to the head. If lying on your back, leg encased in a cast propped on a quilt, didn't make you an invalid, she didn't know what did. But Freeman, as she recalled, had a stubborn nature. She'd certainly seen it at the King wedding.

For an eligible bachelor who owned a house, a mill and two hundred acres of prime land to remain single into his midthirties was almost unheard of among the Amish. Add to that Freeman's rugged good looks and good standing with his bishop and his church community. It made him the catch of the county, several counties for that matter. They could have him. She was a rational person, not a giggling teenager who could be swept off her feet by a pretty face. Freeman liked his own way too much to suit her. Working in his house for two whole weeks wasn't going to be easy, but he or his good looks certainly didn't intimidate her. She'd told Sara she'd take the job and she was a woman of her word.

"I agree. Rest is what he needs." Ivy Kemp came into the house, letting the terrier out the door as she entered. "But he's always been headstrong. Thinking he could tend to that injury to the bull's leg by himself was what got him into trouble in the first place. And not following doctor's orders to stay in bed was what sent him back to the hospital a second time."

"Could you not talk about me as though I'm not here?" Freeman pushed himself up on his elbows. "Two weeks, not a day more, and I'll be on my feet again."

"More like four weeks, according to his doctors," Jehu corrected.

Katie noticed that the blind man had settled himself into a rocker not far from Freeman's bed, removed a string from his pants' pocket, and was absently twisting the string into shapes. She didn't know Jehu well but she'd seen how easily he'd moved around the kitchen and how he turned his face toward each speaker, following the conversation much as a sighted person might. She found him instantly likable.

"Do you know this game?" Jehu asked in Katie's general direction. "Cat's cradle?"

"She doesn't want to play your—"

"I do know it," Katie exclaimed, cutting

Freeman off. "I played it all the time with my father when I was small. I love it."

"Do you know this one?" Jehu grinned, made several quick movements and then held up a new string pattern.

Katie grinned. "That's a cat's eye."

"Easy enough," the older man said, "but how about this one?"

"Uncle Jehu, she didn't come to play children's games." Freeman again. "She was hired to clean up this house."

Katie rolled up her sleeves. "So I was." She glanced Jehu's way. "Later on, I'll show you one you might not know, but right now I better get to work." She turned back in the direction of the kitchen appliances. "I can see I'm desperately needed. There's splatters of milk all over the floor near the stove, and I see ants on the countertop." She removed her black apron and took an everyday white one from the old satchel she'd brought with her.

"It sounds as if Katie has her day's work cut out for her." Sara clapped her hands together. "I'd best get on my way and leave her to it."

Ivy glanced out the window. "I see she's driven her own buggy."

"*Ya,*" Katie confirmed. "We came in two vehicles."

"Katie lives in Apple Valley with her mother

and brother," Sara volunteered. "Too far for her to drive back and forth every day. I have all those extra bedrooms since I added the new addition to my house. It seemed sensible that she should stay with me."

*Especially since my brother just brought home a wife*, Katie thought. Patsy deserved to have the undisputed run of her kitchen. Katie was quite fond of Patsy, who seemed a perfect wife for Isaac. But Katie didn't need to be told that an unmarried sister was definitely a burden on a young couple, so taking this job and living away for a while would give them time to settle into married life. Plus the money she earned by her labor would be put to good use.

"No need for you to run off so quick," Ivy told Sara. "Won't you take a cup of tea over at my place?"

Ivy Kemp was a neat little woman, plump rather than spare, tidy as a wren and just as cheerful. Again, Katie only knew her from intercommunity frolics and fund-raisers, but she seemed pleasant and welcoming.

"Tea?" Jehu got to his feet with more vigor than Katie would expect of a man near seventy. "Tea would hit the spot, Ivy. You don't happen to have any of those raisin bran muffins left over, do you?"

"As a matter of fact, I do." Ivy beamed, head-ing for the door. "But I won't promise they taste as good as they did yesterday when they came out of the oven. You will stay for tea, won't you, Sara? I do love a chance to chat with someone from another church. I hear you made a good match for that new girl with that young man— what's his name…"

In less time than it took Katie to locate a broom, she and Sara had made their goodbyes, and the three older people had left to go next door to the *grossmama haus* for their tea and muffins. Ivy had invited Katie, too, but she'd declined. There was too much to do in Freeman's house and she wanted to get busy.

"I imagine you'll be wanting dinner at noon," she said to Freeman, careful not to look directly at his face and into those striking golden eyes. "Do the doctors have you on a special diet?"

"Oatmeal," he said testily. "I've been eating a lot of oatmeal."

Katie cut her eyes at him. "Odd thing for a sickbed."

"I'm not sick."

"*Ya*, you said that." She opened the refrigerator and grimaced. "I hope the milk and eggs are fresh."

"And why wouldn't they be?"

"If they are, they would be the only thing in that refrigerator that is. It looks as if a bowl of baked beans died in there. The butter is covered in toast crumbs and it looks like there's a hunk of dried up cheese in the back." She wrinkled her nose. "Pretty pitiful fare."

"Spare me your humor." Freeman shut his eyes. "Just cook something other than oatmeal or chicken noodle soup. Anything else. My grandmother has served me so much chicken soup it's a wonder I'm not clucking."

"I'll keep that in mind." She closed the refrigerator door, thinking of the cut-up chicken that Sara had insisted they bring in a cooler. Chicken soup had been one of her options, since she'd known that Freeman was confined to bed and recovering from a bad accident. But she could just as well fry up the chicken with some dumplings. Providing, of course, that there weren't weevils in the flour bin. She'd have to take stock of the pantry and freezer, if Freeman even had a freezer or a flour bin. If they expected her to cook three decent meals a day, she'd have to have the groceries to do it.

She decided that cleaning the refrigerator took precedence over the sticky floor; she'd just sweep now and mop later. Once that was done, she decided she'd better do something about the state of the kitchen table. The tablecloth was stained and could definitely use a washing. Someone had washed dishes that morning and left them on the sideboard to dry, but dirty cups, bowls and silverware littered a side table next to Freeman's bed. A kitchen seemed an odd place for a sick man to have his bed, but she could understand that he might want to be in the center of the home rather than tucked away upstairs alone. And it could be that the bathroom was downstairs. She hadn't been hired for nursing, but, if she knew men, doubtless the sheets could stand laundering.

"That wasn't kind of you," she remarked as she cleared the table and stripped away the soiled tablecloth. "Chastising your uncle when he wanted to show me his string game. You should show more respect for your elders."

Freeman opened one eye. "He's blind, not slipping in his mind. Cat's cradle is for *kinner*. It was him I was thinking of. I wanted to save him embarrassment if you assumed—"

"I hope my mother taught me better than that," Katie interrupted. "I try not to form opinions of people at first glance or to judge them." He didn't answer, and she turned her back to him as she scrubbed the wooden tabletop clean enough to eat off. She would look for a fresh tablecloth, but if none were available, this would suffice until she could do the laundry.

"I don't mean to be rude," Freeman said. He exhaled loudly. "I didn't know you were coming—didn't know any housekeeper was coming. It was my uncle's idea."

"I see." Katie moved on to the refrigerator. The milk container seemed clean and the milk smelled good so she put that on the table with whatever else seemed salvageable. The rest went directly into a bucket to be disposed of. "It's been a good while since anyone did this," she observed.

"It's not something that I can manage with my leg in a cast."

"Six months, I'd guess, since this refrigerator has had a good scrub. You don't need a housekeeper, you need a half dozen of them if you expect me to get this kitchen in shape today."

"It's not *that* bad." He pushed up on his elbows. "Neither Uncle Jehu nor I have gotten sick from the food."

"By the grace of God." The butter went into the bucket, followed by a wilted bunch of beets and a sad tomato. "Do you have a garden?"

Freeman mumbled something about weeds, and she rolled her eyes. Sara's garden was overflowing with produce. She'd bring corn and the makings of a salad tomorrow. A drawer contained butter still in its store wrapping. The date was good, so that went to the table. "Is there anything you're not supposed to eat?" she asked.

"Oatmeal and chicken soup."

She smiled. He was funny; she'd give him that. "So you mentioned."

A few changes of water, a little elbow grease and the refrigerator was empty and clean. Katie started moving items from the table, thinking she'd run outside and get the chicken to let it sit in salted water.

"Butter goes on the middle shelf," Freeman instructed.

She glanced over her shoulder at him. "Not where it says *butter*?" She pointed to the designated bin in the door with the word printed across it.

He scowled. "We like it on the middle shelf."

"But it will stay fresher in the butter bin." She smiled sweetly, left the butter in the door and went back to the table for the milk.

A scratching at the screen door caught her attention and she went to see what was making the noise. When she opened the door, the small brown-and-white rat terrier that Ivy had let out darted in, sniffed her once and then made a beeline for Freeman's bed. "Cute dog."

"His name is Tip." The terrier bounced onto a stool and then leaped the rest of the way onto the bed. He curled under Freeman's hand and butted it with his head until Freeman scratched behind the dog's ears.

Katie watched him cuddle the little terrier. *Freeman couldn't be all bad if the dog liked him.*

She filled the kettle with water and put it on the gas range. She'd seen that there was ice. She'd make iced tea to go with dinner. And if there was going to be chicken and dumplings, she would need to find the proper size pot and give that a good scrub, as well. She planned the menu in her head. Besides the chicken dumplings, she'd have green beans and pickled beets, both canned and carried from Sara's pantry, possibly biscuits and something sweet to top it all off. She'd have to check that weed-choked garden to see if there was something ripe that she could use.

"What are you making for dinner?" Freeman asked.

*Oatmeal*, she wanted to say. But she resisted. It was going to be a long two weeks in Freeman Kemp's company. "I'm not sure yet," she answered sweetly. "It will be a surprise to us both."

"Wonderful," Freeman said dryly. "I can't wait."

Katie swallowed the mirth that rose in her throat. Her employer's nephew might not be the cheeriest companion but at least she wouldn't be bored. Sara had warned her that working in Freeman's house would be a challenge. And there was nothing she liked better.

## Chapter Two

Freeman watched Jehu reach for another biscuit. It was evening and the air was noticeably cooler in the house than it had been in the heat of the afternoon. Being cooped up in the house was making Freeman stir-crazy as it was; the heat seemed to add to his irritability. Thinking back on the day, he hoped he hadn't been too ill-tempered with Katie. He didn't mean to be short with people; it was just his situation that made him crabby. That and the radiating pain in his leg.

Jehu and Ivy were seated at the kitchen table eating leftovers from the midday meal that Katie had cooked. He was lying in his bed, but Katie and Jehu had moved it closer to the table for the noon meal so that he could more easily be included in the conversations, and no one had bothered to push the bed back against the wall. Katie hadn't stayed to have supper with them, though he'd almost hoped she would. It was nice to have someone else to talk to besides his uncle and grandmother. Before Katie left to return to Sara Yoder's, where she was staying, she'd heated up the leftovers, carried them to the table and made him a tray.

"Good biscuits." Jehu felt around for the pint jar of strawberry jam Katie had brought them from her own pantry.

"I thought you must think they were," Ivy remarked. "Since that's your third."

Jehu smiled and nodded. "They are. Aren't they, Freeman?"

"Mmm," Freeman agreed. It was hard to talk with his mouth full. Nodding, he used the rest of his biscuit to sop up the chicken gravy remaining on his plate. He couldn't remember when anything had tasted so good as the meal Katie had served them this afternoon and he was now enjoying it all over again. The green beans were crisp and fresh, and the chicken and dumplings were exactly like those he remembered his mother making. His *grossmama* Ivy had always been dear to him, but no one had ever called her a great cook.

"She's done a marvel on this kitchen," his grandmother pronounced. "She's managed to find the kitchen table under the crumbs and I can walk on this floor without hearing the sand grit under my feet." She looked at Freeman. "We should have got her in here the week you got crushed by that cow."

"It was a bull," Freeman reminded her.

She lifted one shoulder in a *not convinced* gesture. "Not a full grown one."

"Nine hundred pounds, at least." Freeman reached for his coffee. It tasted better than what he usually made. Katie's work, again.

"Pleasant girl, don't you think?" his uncle remarked. For a man who couldn't see, Uncle Jehu had no trouble feeding himself. Somehow, he could eat and drink without getting crumbs in his beard or spots on his clothing. He'd always been a tidy person, almost dapper, if a Plain man could be called dapper. He liked his shirts clean and he wouldn't wear his socks more than once without them being washed. "That Katie Byler."

*"Ya,"* Freeman agreed. The food was certainly a welcome relief from his grandmother's chicken soup, and the kitchen did look better clean, but there was such a thing as overdoing the praise. He wiggled, trying to get in a more comfortable position. He'd had an itch somewhere near the top of his knee, but it was under the heavy cast and he couldn't scratch it. Even when he wasn't in pain there was a dull ache,

but he'd just about gotten used to that. It was the itch that was driving him crazy.

"A hard-working girl who can cook like that will make someone a fine wife," Jehu remarked.

"I was thinking the same thing." Ivy wiped her mouth with a cloth napkin; Katie had found a whole pile of them in one of the cupboards. "Girls like that get snapped up fast. And she's pleasant-looking. Don't you think so, Freeman?"

"What was that?" He'd heard what she said, but didn't really feel comfortable commenting on a woman's looks. Besides, he had a pretty good idea where this conversation was going. They had it all the time, and no matter how often he told Jehu and Ivy he wasn't looking for a wife, they continued looking for him.

"*Pretty.* I said Katie was pretty. Or hadn't you noticed?" She glanced at Uncle Jehu and chuckled. He gave a small sound of amusement as he spooned out the last of the dumplings from the bowl on the table onto his plate, without spilling a drop.

"I thought she might be, just by the sound of her voice," Uncle Jehu said. "You can tell a lot about a person from their voice. Wonder if she's walking out with anybody?"

"Sara says not." His grandmother eyed the

blackberry cobbler on the table. There was nearly half of the baking dish left, plenty for the three of them to enjoy.

Freeman's mouth watered thinking about it. Katie had made it with cinnamon and nutmeg and just the right amount of sugar. Too many women used more sugar than was needed in desserts and hid the taste of the fruit with sweetness.

"This coffee could use a little warming up." Freeman lifted his mug. "I don't want to put anyone to any trouble, but…"

"It won't kill you to drink it like it is," his *grossmama* told him. "Too much hot coffee's not good for broken bones. Raises the heat in the body. Cool's best. Keeps your temperature steady."

Freeman swallowed the rest of his coffee. There was no use in asking Uncle Jehu to warm up his coffee. He'd just side with Ivy. He usually did, Freeman thought, feeling his grumpiness coming on again. The itch on his leg remained persistent, and he wondered if he could run something down inside the cast to scratch it without causing any harm.

"Freeman could do a lot worse," Uncle Jehu went on. "He's not getting any younger."

"Than Katie?" Ivy pursed her mouth. "You're right, Jehu. I don't know why I didn't think of that myself. She'd fit in well here. And it's long past time—"

"Don't talk about me as though I'm not here," Freeman interrupted. "And I'm not courting Katie Byler."

"And what's wrong with her?" Grossmama demanded, turning to him. "She seems a fine possibility to me."

"Absolutely not," Freeman protested, pushing his tray away. "And if this is something you've schemed up with Sara Yoder, you can forget it. Katie may make a great wife for someone else, but not for me."

Katie tossed a handful of weeds into a bucket. "Freeman wasn't as bad as I expected," she answered when Sara asked her how her day had gone. She, Sara and two of the young women who lived at Sara's had come into the vegetable garden after supper to catch up on the weeding. Ellie and Mari had started at the opposite end of the long rows of lima beans, while she and Sara had taken this end, giving the two of them an opportunity to talk privately.

Sara grinned. "I knew you could handle him."

Both she and Sara were barefooted and wearing a headscarf and their oldest dress. The warm soil felt good under Katie's feet. She loved the scents of rich earth and the cheery chorus of birdsong that seemed present in any well-tended garden.

"I think he'd be a good match for someone." Sara used her trowel to chop the sprigs of grass and work up the soil around the base of the lima bean plants. "What with the mill and the farm, he's well set up to provide for a family."

Katie rolled her eyes. "I don't know about that. Any woman who takes Freeman Kemp for a husband is asking for trouble. The man thinks he knows everything. Even when he doesn't. He tried to tell me how to scrub the floor. Can you imagine? And the man doesn't know where butter goes in the refrigerator. And when I tell him the truth of the matter, he gets all cross."

Sara added another handful of weeds to the bucket. They would go into the chicken yard and the scavenging hens would make quick work of them. Nothing ever went to waste on an Amish farm. "Men naturally think they know the best way to do things," she said. "But the wisest of them learn to think before they speak when it comes to women's chores."

"I guess no one ever told Freeman that." Katie tugged at a particularly stubborn pigweed. It came away with a spray of dirt, and she shook it off and added it to the pile. Sara's garden was as tidy as her house, row after row of green peppers, sweet corn, beets, squash and onions. Heavy posts set into the ground made a sturdy support for the wires that supported lima bean vines. Lima beans were one of Katie's favorite vegetables and they were the concern this evening. A summer garden that wasn't worked regularly soon became a tangle of weeds and a haven for bothersome insects.

"Does Freeman seem to be in a lot of pain? Ivy told me the break was a bad one. If he's irritable, that could be the reason," Sara suggested.

"Hard to judge how much pain a person is in." Katie pulled the weed bucket closer to them as they moved down the row. "I think he's more bored from having to stay in bed than anything else. I know it would drive me to distraction if I couldn't be up doing."

"Jehu is nice, though, isn't he?"

"He is. He was very welcoming. He told me not to pay any mind to Freeman's grumpiness. He's an amazing man, really. He knows his way all over that farm, doesn't need a bit of help. I think Freeman said he can see shadows. But you'd never know Jehu was blind the way he moves."

Sara tossed a weed in the bucket. "My cousin Hannah told me that he was a skilled leather worker for years. He still works for the harness shop down his way. Pieces he can stitch from memory."

"It's such a shame that he lost his sight," Katie said.

Sara paused in her weeding and gave Katie a thoughtful look. "It is, but God's will is not always for us to understand. All we can do is accept it and try to make the best of the blessings we have."

From the far end of the rows, Mari and Ellie began to sing "Amazing Grace." Ellie, a little person not more than four feet tall, had a sweet, clear soprano voice, while Mari's rich and powerful alto blended perfectly. Katie smiled, enjoying the sound of their voices in the fading light of the warm evening.

"I had a letter today from Uriah Lambright's aunt." Sara straightened up and rubbed the small of her back. "She says that the family is eager for you to come and visit. Have you given any more thought to considering him?"

"Evening," came a deep male voice.

The four women looked in the direction of the garden gate.

"Ah, James." Sara smiled at the Amish man in his midthirties who had just walked into the garden.

"Katie, do you know James?" Sara asked.

"We've met." She nodded to him. "Evening to you too, James."

James smiled at her and then turned his attention back to Sara. "Can I steal away some of your help?" he asked. "It's such a nice evening, I thought maybe Mari would like to take a ride with me."

Mari came toward them, blushing and brushing dirt from her skirt. Like Katie, Mari was barefoot with only a scarf for a head covering. "I wish you'd given me fair warning," she said, smiling up at James. "I'm not fit to be seen. Can you wait long enough for me to make myself decent and see where Zachary is?"

Zachary was Mari's son, a boy about nine years old. Mari and Zachary were staying with Sara while they made the transition from being English to becoming Amish again. Mari had been raised Amish, but had left the church as a teen and was now returning to the church.

James laughed and used two fingers to push his straw hat higher on his forehead. He was a tall, pleasant-looking man with a quick smile. "I'll wait, but you look fine to me. If you're going to change your clothes, you'd best be quick. Zachary's already in the buggy, and he's trying to convince me that we should go for ice cream."

Mari glanced at Sara who made shooing motions. "Go on, go on," Sara urged. "We can finish up here."

"You're sure?"

"Off with you before I change my mind and put James to work, too," Sara teased.

James swung the gate wide open and Mari hurried to join him. The two walked off, already deep in conversation.

Katie watched them for a minute. She wasn't jealous of Mari's happiness, but she *was* wistful. Katie wanted to marry and have children, but she was beginning to fear it would never happen. She had always assumed God intended her for marriage and a family; it was what an Amish woman was born to. But what if He didn't wish for her to marry?

With a sigh, Katie returned to her work and she and Sara continued weeding until they met Ellie halfway down the row. "You're a fast worker," she told Ellie, observing her work. The soil behind Ellie was as neat and clean as a picture in a garden magazine.

"*Danke.* I try." Ellie's face creased in a genuine smile. "I think the beans at the far end will be ready for picking by tomorrow afternoon."

"If you can wait until after supper, I'd be glad to help you," Katie offered. She liked picking limas, and gardening with other women was always easier than doing it alone. "Willing hands make the work go faster," her mother always said.

"Great," Ellie replied. "It won't take long if we pick them together."

Ellie was the first little person that Katie had ever known, but someone who obviously didn't let her lack of height hinder her. Sara had explained privately that although Ellie had come to Seven Poplars to teach school, Sara had every hope of making a good marriage for her. Ellie was certainly pretty enough to have her choice of men to walk out with, with her blond hair, rosy cheeks, and sparkling blue eyes. Katie had liked her from the first, and she hoped that they might become good friends.

"All right," Sara said, looking across the garden. "I think we've got time to do another row. But there are a lot of full pods on this row. I think we better get to them. Who wants to pick while the other two keep weeding?"

"You pick," Katie told Sara. "I don't mind weeding. It's satisfying to see the results when I'm finished."

*"Ya,"* Ellie said. "Good idea. I can weed, too."

"All right," Sara brushed the dirt off her hands. "It's a bumper crop this summer. Just the right amount of rain, thank the Lord."

"Let's get to it," Katie told Ellie. "Once it

starts to get dark, the mosquitoes will come out, and we'll be fair game, bug spray or no bug spray."

Nodding agreement, Ellie and Katie began to pull weeds again while Sara sought out the plump lima bean pods amid the thick foliage. Conversation came easily to the three of them, and Katie found herself more at ease with Ellie with every passing minute. She was good company, making them double over with laughter at her tales of students. Katie hadn't attended the Seven Poplars schoolhouse, but she'd been there several times for fund-raising events, and Ellie was such a good storyteller that she could picture each event as Ellie related it. Her own school, further south in the county, had been larger, with two rooms rather than one, but otherwise almost identical. Both schools were first through eighth grade and taught by young Amish women.

Sara soon filled her apron with limas and had to return to the house for a basket for them and a second bucket to hold the weeds. When she returned, she brought a quart jar of lemonade to share. Katie and Ellie stopped work long enough to enjoy it before taking up their task again.

"I had a letter from one of my former clients in Wisconsin," Sara said when they'd reached midrow. "Dora Ann Hostetler."

"Do you know her, Ellie?" Katie asked, remembering that Sara had told her that Ellie had come from Wisconsin, too.

Ellie slapped at a hovering horsefly and shook her head. "*Ne*, but Wisconsin's a big state. A lot more Amish communities there than here."

"Anyway," Sara continued. "Dora Ann was a widow with three little girls. A plain woman, but steady, and with a good heart. I found just the man for her last year, a jolly widower with four young boys in need of a mother. She wrote to say that she and Marvin have a new baby boy. She also wanted me to know that her bishop will be visiting in Dover next month, and he'll be preaching here in Seven Poplars. She likes him and assures me that he preaches a fine sermon." She looked at Katie. "Will you be coming to church with us, or going home to your family's church?"

Katie paused in her weeding. "I think I'd like to come with you while I'm here," she said. Sara's mention of the letter from her friend reminded her of the one that Sara had received from Uriah's aunt. "You started to tell me earlier about the note from Uriah's family," she reminded.

"Yes, but…" Sara hesitated. "Would you rather discuss that in private?"

"*Ne*, I don't mind." Katie chuckled. "Actually, I'd like to hear Ellie's opinion."

Sara placed her basket, now nearly full of lima beans, on the ground. "Katie has an interested suitor," she explained to Ellie. "A young man who used to be a neighbor to her family here in Kent County."

"Uriah, his parents and brothers and sisters moved to Kentucky years ago," Katie said as she tamped down the weeds in the bucket to make room for more. "Uriah is the oldest."

"The family has a farm and a sawmill in Kentucky," Sara added. She continued searching for ripe beans. "Uriah's father made initial contact with me a few weeks ago about the possibility of making a match for his son with Katie."

Katie threw Ellie a wry look. "It was the *father* who asked about me, mind you, not Uriah."

Ellie sat back on her heels and glanced from Katie to Sara and back to Katie. "So you know Uriah from when you were younger?"

Katie nodded. "They left when we were twelve, maybe thirteen. He was in the same school year as I was. They come back every year or so to see family so I've seen him a few times over the last few years."

"Then you must have some idea of what you

think of him," Ellie said. "Is he someone you can imagine yourself married to?"

Katie sighed. "That's the problem. I don't know. I mean, I know he's a good person and strong in his faith. He's shy; he's always been shy. I suppose that's why his father made the inquiry. And there's nothing *wrong* with him." She sighed again.

"Well, is he hardworking? Does he have any bad habits? Those are the kinds of questions I think you need to ask yourself." Ellie worked up the ground around the base of a plant. "But I guess the important thing is, do you like him?"

Katie thought for a minute. "I do like him," she said, then she wrinkled her nose. "I just never thought of him as a possible husband. He was just sort of always…there."

"So what you're saying is what?" Ellie asked. "Boring?"

"Ellie!" Sara's admonition was only half-serious. "What way is that to talk of a man you don't even know?"

"No…I wouldn't call Uriah boring," Katie answered. "He's serious, but not, you know, not deadly serious." She thought for a minute. "And he likes dogs. He always had a dog."

Ellie laughed merrily. "Now *there's* a recommendation for a husband. Or it would be if you were a dog." She shook her head. "It doesn't sound as if you're too excited about this offer. So there's got to be something about him that you don't like or you'd be more enthusiastic about the idea." She hesitated. "I know looks shouldn't matter to us, but...do you find him unattractive?"

*"Ne,"* Katie insisted. "It's not like that. He isn't...ugly. He's...I don't know...average-looking, I suppose, and he has nice teeth."

Ellie giggled. "Nice teeth. There's a plus." She shook the dirt off a weed and tossed it playfully at Katie. "If I were you, I wouldn't be able to contain myself. Not boring, nice teeth, and too shy to come and check you out for himself. Yup. That's the man for you."

Katie and Ellie both laughed.

"Put that talk by," Sara chided, in earnest this time. "Uriah Lambright is a respectable candidate. I would have never brought him up to Katie if I didn't think so. His aunt tells me that he's building a house for his new bride, and that he's well thought of in his community. Not every worthy bachelor is forward around the opposite sex. And since Katie says that she has no objections to taking inquiries further, that's exactly what I'm doing."

"Could you do that?" Ellie asked Katie. "Marry someone that you weren't strongly attracted to? I know I couldn't. When I choose a husband, if I ever do, I want it to be someone I can love." She wrapped her arms around her tiny waist. "Someone I just couldn't live without."

"Some marriages do start with romance," Sara conceded, "but not all of them. I've arranged many matches between total strangers. There must be respect and liking, and then often, if both parties want the partnership to be successful, love follows."

"My mother says the same thing." Ellie got to her feet and brushed the dirt off the back of her dress. "She tells me that if I wait for romantic love, I may end up an old maid, caring for other people's babies and sitting at other women's tables."

"That's exactly what I'm afraid of," Katie agreed. "That's why I know I should take the Lambrights' offer seriously. I want romance. I want love. But what if that's not what God intends for me?" Without another weed in sight, she rose to her feet, too. "I'm not saying I'm ready to say *ya* to Uriah, but neither am I willing to just say no outright. What if he *is* the person God intends for me to wed? And so far, he's the only one who's shown any interest other than the occasional ride in a buggy home from a singing."

"I don't know." Ellie turned thoughtful. "I

understand what you're saying, but I think I hear a *but* there." She looked up at Katie. "You're saying all the right things, but I think there has to be something about this Uriah that makes you cautious."

"I suppose it's that I'm not convinced that Uriah is interested in me," Katie admitted readily. "He hasn't written, and he hasn't come to see me. What if his family is more interested in this match than he is? I know that his parents and his grandmother always liked me, but I wouldn't be marrying them. What if Uriah's being pushed into this match?"

"That's always a possibility," Sara agreed. "And if that's the case, then I certainly wouldn't advise you to accept his offer of courtship. But you don't know the facts yet. Both you and Ellie are young, and the young tend to believe they have all the answers." She met Katie's gaze, waggling her finger at her. "I will tell you this. More than one young woman has broken her own heart waiting for the perfect man to appear from far off, while the one she should have chosen—" she pointed at Katie "—was standing right in front of her."

# Chapter Three

There were no complaints from Freeman on the meal Katie cooked the following morning, and if not jovial, he was at least polite to her. Jehu had a third helping of bacon and toast, and Freeman did admit that her meal was an improvement over his grandmother's oatmeal.

Ivy hadn't come over to the big house yet; presumably, the older woman was enjoying a respite from the men and eating her preferred breakfast. Still, Katie missed Ivy's cheerful presence at the table. She liked Ivy's no-nonsense way of dealing with the men, especially Freeman, and she reminded Katie of her own *grossmama,* Mary Byler, who'd passed away several winters earlier.

Once everyone had eaten and the dishes were washed and put away, Jehu and the dog went to the mill and Katie turned to the laundry.

"When is the last time those sheets of yours were washed?" she asked Freeman.

He scowled at her. "Not long."

"How long exactly?" she persisted.

"Probably when I came home from the hospital."

She sniffed in disapproval and pursed her lips. "It won't do, you know. Lying on dirty linens."

His dark eyes narrowed. They were still beautiful eyes, but the expression was peevish and resentful, like an adolescent who'd been told he couldn't go fishing with his friends but had to stay home and clean the chicken coop. "And how do you suggest that I change and wash these sheets?"

"Don't be surly," she scolded. "I'll do the washing, but you'll have to get out of bed so that I can strip it."

Freeman rapped on his cast with a fist. "Doctor says that the leg has to remain elevated."

Katie sighed with impatience. "We're both intelligent people. I think we can figure out a solution." The previous day, when she'd first come in, she'd noticed a wheelchair folded up and resting against the wall, the packing strap still wrapped around it. Clearly, Freeman had never used the chair. Resolutely prepared for resistance, she approached the bed. "Are you decent?"

"I should hope so. I try to do the right thing."

It took all of her willpower not to show her exasperation. He was wearing a light blue shirt, wrinkled but clean, rather than the sleeveless T-shirt he'd worn the day before. She'd wanted to know if he had trousers on under the sheet and blankets. And she had the feeling that he knew exactly what she'd been asking and chose to be difficult. "You know what I mean," she said briskly. "Are you wearing anything other than your skin below your waist?"

Two spots of color glowed through the dark stubble on his cheeks. *"Ya,"* he muttered. "Grossmama cut a leg off a pair of my pants so I could pull them on over the cast. The traveling nurse was coming to the house when I first got home from the hospital so—" He scowled at her, his blush becoming even more evident. "Why would you need to know what I have on under my sheet?"

Katie pursed her lips and regarded him with the same expression she used with her brothers when they were being impossible. "Because I need to change those sheets, and I can't get you out of the bed and into the wheelchair without your cooperation." She folded her arms resolutely. "You're certainly too heavy for me to carry, but if you're a miller, I'd guess that you have a lot of strength in your upper body. If I bring that wheelchair up beside the bed, can you use your arms to maneuver into it?"

"Didn't say yet that I want to get out of bed," he protested.

She could tell it wasn't much of an argument, more for show than anything else. "Of course you want to get up. You'd have to be thick-headed to want to stay there like a lump of coal." She tilted her head, softening her voice. "And, Freeman, you're anything but slow-witted if I'm any judge."

"I suppose I could manage to heave myself into the thing," he said grudgingly. "I hadn't decided if I was keeping it, though. Wheel-chairs are expensive. I'll be back on my feet soon enough and—"

"It's going to be weeks before you're back on your feet," she interrupted. "Too long for you to lie in that bed." She stared down at him and he stared up at her and it occurred to her that they could possibly be there all day just wait-ing to see who would bend first.

He did.

"Fine," he finally muttered. "But, I warn you, there aren't any more sheets in the house to fit this size bed. Am I supposed to sit in that contraption all day while you do the laundry and hang it out to dry?"

She tried not to show how amused she was. Stubborn, the man was as stubborn as a broody hen refusing to budge off a clutch of wooden eggs. She suspected he wanted to be out of that bed more than she wanted him to do it, but he wasn't going to make it easy for her. "You must have other sheets. In a linen closet?"

He nodded. "But I just told you. They won't fit. They're for larger beds than this."

"That's women's matters. No need for you to worry yourself over it." She gave him a sympathetic look. "I'm sure it will be painful...moving from the bed to the chair. If it really is too much, just say so."

Again, the scowl. "I'm not afraid of a little pain."

She went to the wheelchair, cut the plastic shipping strap with scissors and began to unfold it. "While you're out of bed, maybe you could find your razor. You're badly in need of a shave."

Being unmarried, Freeman should have been clean-shaven. Either he or someone had shaved him in the last week, but he had at least a five-day growth of reddish-brown beard. His hair was too long. Getting him shaven and onto clean sheets would be a small victory. And she'd found with her father and brothers that small steps worked best with men. You had to make them think ideas were their own. Otherwise, they tended to balk and turn mulish. She hesitated, and then suggested, "I could do it for you, if you like. My brother, Little Joe, broke two fingers on his right hand once and I—"

"I can shave myself. It's my leg that's broken, not my hand."

When she glanced back to the bed, Freeman was looking at the wheelchair with obvious apprehension. She understood his hesitation, but she truly did think his upper body was strong enough to move himself safely into the wheelchair. "If you did get in the chair, you could go out on the porch easy enough," she said with genuine kindness. "It's a beautiful day. You must be going mad as May butter staring at these kitchen walls."

"I am," he admitted.

Her irritation was fading fast. Freeman was a challenge. He might be prickly, but he was interesting. Being with him kept her on her toes and anything but bored. It must take a lot of energy for him to pretend to be so grumpy. And she suspected it wasn't his true nature. "What was that?" she teased.

His high brow furrowed. "I *said* I am. I'm

tired of staring at this room. A house is no place for a man in midmorning."

"Which is our best reason for getting you out of that bed. An easy mind makes for quicker healing." She brought the wheelchair to the side of the bed. "Careful," she warned. "Let me help you."

"*Ne*. You steady the chair so it doesn't roll."

"It won't. I've put the brakes on."

"Stand aside, then, and let me do it by myself." Slowly, pale and with sweat breaking out on his forehead, Freeman managed the gap from the bed to the chair. Katie knew that it must have hurt him, but he didn't make a sound, and finished sitting upright with a look of pure satisfaction on his face.

"Wonderful," she said, squeezing her hands together. She raised the leg rest and carefully propped his cast on it. Then she released the brake and pushed him out of the kitchen and down the short hall to the bathroom. He told her where to find his razor and shaving cream. "You won't be able to see into the mirror," she said, handing him a washcloth and draping a towel around his neck. This mirror was small and fixed to the wall over the sink. "Is there another mirror I could bring in here?"

"I don't need your help. Just hand me my razor and soap and brush from over there," he said, pointing to a pretty old oak dresser that she suspected held towels and the like. "I've done this hundreds of times. I can manage without the mirror."

"If you'll tell me where to find scissors, I could trim the back of your hair. That's not something you can do yourself," she offered, putting his things on the edge of the sink.

"My hair is fine. Now go change those sheets you've been fussing about."

She made no argument but went and located a linen closet at the top of the stairs. As Freeman had said, it had sheets for double beds, but she could easily tuck the excess under the mattress. The important thing was that the sheets were clean. They would do for now. Next time, she would have freshly washed and line-dried linen to go on his bed, provided he didn't fire her first.

When she finished the task and returned to the bathroom, she found him still sitting at the sink, shaving cream on his face and a razor in his hand. There were uneven patches of beard on his cheeks and a trickle of blood down his chin. Wordlessly, he handed the razor to her, grimaced, and clenched his eyes shut. She ran hot water on the washcloth, twisted it until the excess water ran out, and pressed it over his face.

She'd said that shaving Freeman would be no different that shaving her brothers, but as she stood there looking at him, she realized it was. It was very different. She had to steady her hands as she removed the washcloth and began with more shaving cream. Her pulse quickened, and she felt a warm flush beneath her skin.

Shaving Freeman was more intimate than she'd supposed it would be and she was thankful that his dark eyes were closed. The act bordered on inappropriate behavior between an unmarried man and woman, but neither of them intended it to be anything other than what it was. She'd offered with the best of intentions and backing down now would be worse than going through with it, wouldn't it?

But what if her hands trembled and she cut him? How would she explain that?

She took a deep breath and plunged forward, silently praying, *Don't let my hand slip. Please, don't let him see how nervous I am.* The small curling hairs at the nape of her neck grew damp and her knees felt weak, but she kept sliding the razor down the smooth plane of his cheek. The blade was sharp, and Freeman held perfectly still. If he'd moved, even a fraction of an inch, she knew that the blade would break his skin, but he didn't, and she managed to finish without disgracing herself.

"All done." Heady with success, she handed him the wet washcloth. "See, it wasn't that bad, was it?"

"Thank you." He wiped his face and opened his eyes.

"I could still do something with your hair," she offered.

He wiped a last bit of shaving cream from his chin and tossed the washcloth in the sink. "Quit while you're ahead, woman."

She laughed. "You do look a lot better." And he did, more than better. Shaggy hair brushing his shirt collar or not, he had the kind of good looks that cautious mothers warned their daughters against. And with good reason, she thought, as she locked her shaking hands behind her back.

"I'm not a vain man."

She couldn't hide a mischievous grin. *"Ne?"* She thought that he wasn't telling the exact truth. In her mind, most men were as vain as any woman. They just hid it better. And Freeman had more reason than most to take pride in his looks.

"I'm a Plain man. I have more on my mind than my appearance."

"I can see that," she agreed. "But no one said that a clean and tidy man was an offense to the church."

He fixed her with those lingering brown eyes, eyes that were not as full of disapproval as they had been. "Do you have an answer for everything?" he asked. But she sensed that he was making an effort at humor rather than being sarcastic.

"I try." She nodded. "Now I'll leave you to finish washing up. Call when you need me to bring you back out to the kitchen."

"I think I can push myself," he grumbled.

Smiling, she left him to go throw the sheets in the wash.

She'd just started mixing a batch of cornbread when Freeman came rolling slowly down the hall. He looked pale, as if he'd run a long distance. She could tell he was in pain, but she didn't say anything about it. "Do you think you could peel potatoes for me?"

"I suppose I could," he said. "Isn't it too early to be starting the midday meal?"

"Too early for cooking. Not too early for starting the preparation. I've lots to do this morning, and you have to be organized to get meals on the table on time and still get the rest of your work done."

"Organization is a good thing," he agreed. "Not many people understand that. They waste hours that could go to good purpose."

"Mmm." She brought him a large stainless

steel bowl, a paring knife, and the potatoes. "If you peel these, I'll cut them up and put them in salted water, ready to cook when it gets closer to mealtime."

"My mother was a good cook," he said.

"Mine, too. Better than me."

"She's still with you, isn't she?"

"*Ya*, thanks be to God. We lost my father a few years ago, but we were fortunate to have him as long as we did. *Dat* had five heart surgeries, starting when he was a baby. He was never strong, but he lived a full life, and he and my mother were happy together."

"It's important, having parents who cared for each other. Mine did, too. They died too soon. An accident." He shook his head, and she saw the gleam of moisture in his eyes. "I'd rather not talk about it."

Then why did he bring it up, she wondered. But she was glad that he had, felt that it was a positive step in their relationship. If she was going to work here, for the next two weeks, it would be better if they weren't always butting heads.

"Do you fish?" he asked.

"What?" She'd been thinking about what he'd said about his parents and hadn't been giving him her full attention. "Do I like fish? To eat?"

"*Ya*, to eat. But I meant to catch. I like fishing. It's what I usually do on summer evenings. We have big bass in the millpond, catfish, perch, as well as sunnies."

"I do like fishing," she said. "And crabbing. My *dat* used to take us to Leipsic. We'd crab off the bridge there. And fish, too, but we never caught many."

"It takes patience and know-how. Bass, especially, are clever. But very tasty. I use artificial lures for them."

Jehu strolled in, sniffing the air. "Making corn fritters?"

"Cornbread," Katie said.

"I love cornbread." He went to the table and sat down near Freeman. "Laundry going, I hear. You've been busy, Katie." He pulled his cat's cradle string out of his pocket. "Learned a new one this morning. From Shad, of all people. Shad is Freeman's apprentice. Good boy, hard worker."

"I wouldn't say apprentice," Freeman corrected. "Shad's got a long way to go before he can call himself a miller. Thinks too much of himself, that boy. Headstrong."

"Sounds likes somebody else I know," Jehu said. He turned his head in Freeman's direction. "Sounds like you got him up and out of that bed. And shaved, too, if I'm not mistaken.

I smell your shaving cream." He turned toward the sink where Katie was grating a cabbage she'd brought from Sara's garden. "You're a good influence on him, Katie. Best thing in the world for him. Get out of bed, cleaned up, and stop feeling sorry for himself."

The screen door squeaked and Ivy joined them. The terrier ran across the kitchen and leaped up on the newly-made bed. "What are you up to, Katie? Don't tell me you're already starting dinner?" She smiled warmly. "Freeman, look at you. Up and shaved. I think I know who to give credit to for this."

Freeman grimaced, picking up another potato to peel. "Morning, Grossmama. I'm feeling better, thank you."

"I can see that for myself," she answered crisply. "And she's put you to work."

"I couldn't find a vegetable peeler," Katie said. "Just a paring knife."

"You won't, not in this house. I've got one if you need to borrow it. Help yourself." She picked up one of the potatoes Freeman had peeled. "Not bad," she said, "not good, but not bad. Be more careful. Waste not." She turned back to Katie. "I just made a fresh pot of tea, and I was hoping that you'd come to my house and have some with me."

"I don't know," Katie hemmed. "I've got a lot to do."

"It'll wait," Ivy told her, giving a wave. "Come on. We can get to know each other." She looked up at Katie. "You know you want to."

"You should go, Katie," Jehu encouraged. "I'll keep an eye on Trouble, here." He tipped his head in Freeman's direction.

Katie was torn. She *did* have a lot to do, but it seemed important to Ivy that they share a pot of tea. And God didn't put them on the earth just to sweep and wash, did He? In the end, people mattered more than chores. It was something her mother, though a hard worker, had instilled in her young. "Oh…why not?" she conceded.

"I'd like some tea," Freeman said. "But I like mine cold. The doctor said I should drink lots of fluids." He frowned. "Katie's busy. We didn't hire her to sit and drink tea. She has chores to do, and we were having a serious conversation about—"

"Fishing," his uncle supplied with a grin. "Which means that she's certainly earned a break. Go along with Ivy, Katie. Enjoy your tea. I'll make Grumpy his iced tea. Just as soon as he finishes peeling the potatoes."

# Chapter Four

"Come along, dear. We'll have a cup of tea and get to know each other better." Ivy's invitation was as warm and welcoming as her smile as she led Katie down the walkway between the two houses.

The *grossmama haus* stood under the trees on the far side of the farmhouse where Freeman and Jehu lived. To reach Ivy's place, she and Katie had only to follow the brick path from Freeman's porch to a white picket fence. There, a blue gate opened to a small yard filled with a riot of blooming flowers and decorative shrubs. Katie counted at least a dozen different blooming perennials she could put names to and several she couldn't. There were climbing roses, hydrangea, hollyhocks and lilies, so many flowers that barely a patch of green lawn was visible.

Hummingbird feeders hung on either side of the front door, and the air was filled with the exciting sounds of the tiny, iridescent-feathered creatures, as well as the buzz of honeybees and the chattering voice of a wren. "How beautiful," Katie said. "Your flowers."

"They're God's gift to us and a constant joy to me," Ivy said. "They ask only for sunshine and rain and a little care against the weeds and they bloom their hearts out for us. I'm so pleased that you like my garden. Are you interested in flowers?" She pushed open the front door, ushering Katie into a combined kitchen and sitting room.

Everything inside was neat and orderly. The furnishings were simple: a sofa, an easy chair, a rocker and a round oak table and matching chairs. The appliances were small but new, and they fit perfectly into the small, cheerful cottage with its large windows and hardwood flooring. Colorful family trees, cross-stitch Bible verses and a calendar hung on the walls. A sewing basket sat by the rocker, and a copy of the Amish newspaper, *The Budget*, lay open on the sofa. In the center of the table rested a blue pottery teapot, a sugar bowl and pitcher, with two cups and saucers.

"I do love my tea, even on a warm day," Ivy said. "I hope you do, too. Coffee is invigorating, but tea calms the mind and spirit." She waved toward the table. "Please, sit down."

Katie took a seat at the table. "Your house is lovely."

"It's wonderful, isn't it? Freeman had it built for me just last year. It's the first new home I've ever lived in. I grew up in an old farmhouse near Lancaster, and then when I married Freeman's grandfather, I came here to the millhouse as a bride. I never had cause to complain, but I do love my *grossmama haus*. It's warm in winter, my stove doesn't smoke and the floors don't creak."

Ivy poured tea into one of the cups and handed it to her. Even Ivy's dishes showed her love of flowers. The cup and saucer were bright with green leaves and purple violets. "But I'm running on. It comes of living alone, I think. It's not easy, you know. I fear that when I do have company I never give them a chance to get a word in." Her speech was grandmotherly, but her eyes, alert and missing nothing, gave evidence of an intelligent and still vibrant woman. She smiled again, disarmingly. "So, tell me about your family, Katie. Do you have brothers and sisters?"

"Two brothers," she answered. "I'm the youngest. There's Isaac. He's the oldest and was named after my father. Isaac has the family farm, and then there's Robert, who lives across the road from us. Our family is small, but close. Isaac and Robert were always inseparable."

"Two brothers," Ivy echoed. "I always wanted brothers. I come from a small family myself. My mother had only two of us that lived past babyhood, my sister and me. My father longed so for sons, but it wasn't to be."

Katie stirred milk into her tea. "My father and mother were hoping for a girl. There hadn't been any girls born in my father's family for two generations."

"Funny isn't it, how patterns repeat in families? My husband was an only child and while we hoped for a large family, we were blessed with only the one child as well." She looked at the window and sighed. "I always imagined having a wealth of grandbabies to hug and fuss over, but there was only Freeman. With two sons married, I suppose your fortunate mother has grandchildren."

"Two so far, Robert's. Isaac just married. It's partially why I took this job. I really like Patsy, and I thought she should have time to settle into her home without a third woman in the house. Mother lives with us, as well. We lost my father a few years back."

"I heard about that, and I'm so sorry. Your brother Robert has children?"

"Twins. Boys. Just learning to walk. I adore them."

"So you're fond of children?"

"I am."

"I hope when you marry that you are blessed with more than a single child. It's hard not to indulge them. But Freeman's father was a precious child and a good man. He never gave us a night's worry. I know he's safe with the Lord, but losing him and Freeman's mother in that accident was a terrible loss. She was like a daughter to me."

"Freeman mentioned that they had died."

"A boating accident. They were fishing on the Susquehanna. She was from Lancaster County, and her uncle took them out. We don't know what happened. They may have struck a rock. They say the currents are dangerous. I was so distraught that the weight of it fell on Freeman's shoulders."

"I'm so sorry."

Ivy sighed. "Death is part of life. But a mother should never have to bury her child. I don't care what the bishop says. It goes against everything that is right and natural." She ran her fingertips absently along the edge of her saucer. "You must think my faith is weak, to talk so."

*"Ne,"* Katie assured her. "I can't imagine how difficult it would be to lose both a husband and your only child."

Ivy swallowed, her eyes, so much like Freeman's, sparkled with tears unshed. "It was… very hard. They say it gets easier with time and prayer, but some days…" She broke off and looked out the window. A silence stretched between them, but it was one of shared loss rather than awkwardness. After a moment or two, she glanced at Katie and brightened. "How old are you?"

Katie thought it was an odd question. Why did Ivy care how old the housekeeper was? But she wasn't offended in any way. "Twenty-three," she answered. "Twenty-four soon."

"And have you been baptized into the church?"

"I have. Last summer."

"Good." Ivy nodded her approval. "I cannot imagine living through such loss without the knowledge that those I love are forever beyond pain and sickness and that I will someday see them again."

"That's true," Katie said. "I feel the same way about my father. I miss him terribly, but he suffered from his condition, and now he is at peace."

"*Ya.* I do believe that."

"And you aren't alone," Katie said. "You still have Freeman," she said. "And, as you say, he's a good man. He must be a great comfort to you."

"He is." Ivy sighed. "He always has been. Do you see what expense he went to building this house for me? I didn't need anything so fancy, but I love it. And I have two bedrooms, when one should have been plenty, so if you ever want to stay over, you're welcome to stay here with me."

"That's very kind of you," Katie said.

"I'm not saying that my Freeman is without his faults. I wouldn't want you to think that I'm as blind as Jehu. I'm afraid we did spoil him as a child. He's a good boy, and I love him dearly, but he *is* fond of having his own way. Like his father and grandfather before him, there's only one way to do something, and that's the Kemp way."

Katie smiled. "My brothers have accused me of always wanting things done the *Katie* way. They say I'm stubborn, but if my way is the best way, why should I change to please someone else? So long as the job gets done right and as quickly as needed?"

"Men do hate having women show them how to do something easier," Ivy said. "I'm afraid it's born in them. In some ways, I don't believe any of them ever grow up. They're like little boys in grownup clothing." She chuckled. "They never get past the age of wanting a woman to take care of them and clean up after them."

"Speaking of which, I'd best get back to my chores." Katie started to rise. "The tea was delicious, but if we're to have our midday meal on time, I should go."

"Please, don't go yet," Ivy said. "I promise, no more sad talk. I'm ashamed of myself that I invited you to come and chat and then went on about my losses. I'm a poor hostess."

*"Ne,"* Katie insisted. "I don't mind. I'm glad that you felt you could share your heartache with me. My mother is a good person, and we're very close. I couldn't ask for a better parent, but she doesn't talk about such things… about missing my father. She was never one to talk about her feelings. She says that we should keep such thoughts private. What you said about it being hard to accept…I feel the same way." She reached out and squeezed Ivy's hand. "It eases my heart to know that I'm not the only one who wants to put her sorrows into words. But I better go." She gave a small sound of amusement as she stood. "As Freeman said, I'm not being paid to sit and drink tea. I came

to his house to work, and if his meal is late, you know he'll fuss."

"Let him fuss," Ivy insisted. "Sit down and have another cup of tea and tell me all about this offer of marriage you have from Kentucky that Sara was telling me about. If my grandson has something to say about what time his dinner goes on the table, he can say it to me because I'm keeping you here for my own pleasure. Besides…" She shrugged and mischief lit her eyes. "Sometimes, it's good for a man to wait on a woman."

"She's late, isn't she?" Freeman asked aloud, directing his question to no one in particular.

He was sure that it had been well before eight when Katie arrived the morning before. He'd slept well the previous night and had awakened at the first rooster crow. He'd gotten himself up and into the wheelchair and washed, shaved and dressed himself so that Katie would have no reason to criticize him. Now he was resting in the bed, waiting for her.

It seemed as if he'd been waiting for her to arrive for hours. He thought maybe they could sit on the porch this morning and shell the lima beans Jehu had brought in from the garden the night before. Freeman was looking forward to getting out of the house, if only just to the porch. He'd have a view of the mill from there and he could see the height of the water in the smaller overflow pond. Anything but staring at this kitchen all day, he thought.

He glanced at the mantel clock again and found only four minutes had passed since he last looked. "She was here earlier yesterday, I'm sure of it."

"Eight." Jehu held out a mug of coffee. "No reason to think Katie won't be here on time this morning." How he managed to pour coffee and carry it across the room without spilling a drop when he was blind as a scarecrow, Freeman couldn't imagine. "Drink this and keep your trousers on. It will hold you until breakfast."

"If we ever get it," Freeman grumbled. "*Danke.* I appreciate it." He took a sip of the coffee. As usual, Jehu had forgotten to add milk, but Freeman wouldn't mention it. He'd drink it black, one more indignity for a man laid low by his own stupidity. All he had had to do was wait until Shad arrived to help him with the bull. But no, he had to do it himself. Couldn't wait. Couldn't ask for help. He'd been so sure that he could manage the half-wild animal, and the bull had made a sideways jump and knocked him against the fence as easily as if he was a ten-year-old child. He couldn't even blame the animal. The beast hadn't intended to hurt him. He was simply reacting out of panic. The other men, when they'd caught up with him, had easily surrounded it and driven it into a neighbor's pasture where they'd been able to get a rope on it.

He couldn't have picked a worse time to get laid up. Shad was just beginning to understand the milling process. He didn't know the first thing about controlling the flow of water out of the millpond, and the financial end of the business was beyond him. Everything was done on the computer: all the billings, delivery schedules, and bookkeeping. And the computer was in the mill office, seventy-five yards away, but it might have been seventy-five miles for all his ability to get there and use it. There was no electricity in the house, no telephone. They were in the office, strictly for business and emergencies, and closely watched by the local deacon, who was suspicious of all such worldly electronics.

His grandmother could operate the old-fashioned, manual cash register. She could sell one- and five-pound sacks of wheat and rye flour to the customers, but she didn't have the faintest idea how to make a spreadsheet or send and receive email and she hadn't had much success motivating Shad to take initiative in the actual milling process.

What was happening to the family business while he was flat on his back weighed heavier on him than the pain of his leg, and Katie Byler disturbed him even further. Although…he had to admit she'd set the kitchen to rights, and he'd slept a lot better on clean sheets. He wasn't a slovenly man, and clean clothes and a shave made him feel more like himself. But he liked things done a certain way, and she didn't seem to understand that although he was temporarily incapacitated, he was still master of this house.

Not that he was an unreasonable man. He could see now that, considering the circumstances, having Katie come was a good idea. He'd set his mind to being more open to having this stranger in his house for a few days. There was no doubt that she had shaken his self-absorption and given him something to think about other than his own problems. She was an excellent cook, and she wasn't exactly hard to look at. To be truthful, Katie was more than average in appearance. The golden-blond locks that curled around an oval face, even features, and wide, thick-lashed blue eyes were enough to make any man look at her twice. A few golden freckles dusted her nose and cheekbones, but they didn't mar her fair German complexion; they only added to her beauty.

Freeman grimaced. He couldn't fault her looks. It was Katie's unnatural nature that made her less than what a proper woman should be. She was too quick to question a man's judgment, and too set in her own ways. No wonder she had to resort to a matchmaker to find a husband.

Not that he hadn't done the same, he grudgingly conceded. Several years earlier, he'd tired of his grandmother's murmuring about him being past time to wed. So, he'd consulted with a matchmaker to try and find a suitable wife. Not Sara Yoder, but a woman in Lancaster. Sara had not yet come to live in Seven Poplars, or he would have gone to her. It would have been easier face-to-face than doing everything by letter.

It turned out the matchmaker didn't have any more success than he'd had on his own. The three girls she'd suggested were all wrong. Different reasons, but all wrong for him. Of course, he'd found the right woman years ago, and she'd chosen another. It had been a bitter pill to swallow, but he'd had to accept it. He knew that his grandmother was eager for him to marry and give her great-grandchildren, but he wasn't going to just settle. If he couldn't find the right woman, one who made him feel eight feet tall, he'd remain a bachelor.

The mantel clock began to chime. "Eight o'clock. That does it," Freeman declared. "She's late. And what are we supposed to—"

"Good morning!" Katie called out as she came into the kitchen, eyes sparkling with energy, arms full, and cheeks pink with ruddy health. She set a covered basket on the table and whisked off the woven lid. She was wearing a dark green dress that fell a few inches below her knees, dark stockings and low, black sneakers. "Sara made blueberry pancakes this morning, and she had extra," Katie proclaimed. "I packed hot water bottles around them to keep them warm. And I've got real maple syrup and blueberry compote." She removed a white apron from her basket, shook it out, and tied it around her waist. "I'm going to just pop them in the oven for a few minutes and then they'll be ready."

After breakfast, Freeman sat in the bed, eyeing the porch. He wondered if maybe he could walk the couple of feet out the door and to a chair, with his uncle's assistance. It would just make him feel better. He'd only been using the wheelchair three days but he was already sick of it.

Katie wouldn't have it, though.

"Absolutely not," she declared. "You're still supposed to be keeping your leg elevated. You're going to be off your feet for at least six weeks—"

"That's an exaggeration. The doctor never said six weeks," Freeman protested. He'd probably be bankrupt by then. Shad would have done something stupid with the mill mechanism and the wheels would stop turning. Customers would start taking their business someplace else. He couldn't afford six weeks off from work.

"Was it six?" Uncle Jehu asked. "I thought it was seven weeks."

Freeman gritted his teeth, even though he knew from his uncle's voice that he was just teasing. You would think that a man's uncle would take his side once in a while instead of forever siding with either Grossmama or Katie. Men were supposed to stick together.

Ignoring the both of them, Katie sat down in the wheelchair and maneuvered it around the kitchen table. Then she leaned back, bringing the front end up. It was all Freeman could do not to warn her to be careful. He didn't want her taking a spill.

"This is kind of fun." She lifted one footrest and propped up her leg. "And this will keep your leg elevated just as the doctor ordered. I can put a pillow under, if need be."

"I suppose you're right," he said, begrudgingly. If he could get around by himself, he guessed he could deal with the wheelchair for a few days. Anything would be better than lying flat on his back in that bed another day. "I got up myself this morning."

"That's good," Katie said. She moved to a kitchen chair and began to remove her shoes and stockings.

"Why are you doing that?" He should have looked away, but he didn't. If she was bold enough to roll down her stockings in front of a man, she couldn't blame him if he watched.

"I mean to do some heavy cleaning. And bare feet wash easier than stockings." She tucked her stockings into her shoes and slid them under the chair and brought the wheelchair to the side of his bed. "Ready?"

He tried not to grumble as she held the chair so that he could get off the bed and into it. And he only gave a small groan as she lifted his bad leg onto the footrest.

"Your hair still needs trimming," she said, hands on her hips, regarding him critically. "Are you certain you don't want me to cut it for you?"

"I'll think about it."

She smiled. "Good. Want to go out on the porch? I saw some things out there that need doing. I thought I might start there this morning."

Freeman slowly made his way out onto the porch to where he could see the pond and the front of the mill. She brought him a newspaper, a recent issue of *Farm Journal*, and a copy of *National Geographic* from her bag. "I don't know if you like to read," she said, almost shyly, "but I saw the old newspapers stacked up in that box beside the door, here on the porch, so I thought you must read them."

"I do like to read in the evening," he said, giving her a genuine smile. "When my chores for the day are finished. But where did you get these magazines? They aren't ours."

"My brother Robert takes the *Farm Journal* and he saves them for me. It's last month's, but there are some good articles."

"And the *National Geographic*?"

She colored a faint shade of pink. "Mine. I know it isn't accepted reading for most Amish, but there are good articles about African wildlife and killer whales and all sorts of topics that even the deacon couldn't object to."

"So you're a reader, too." He studied her closely. He wouldn't have thought her a reader. Most Amish weren't, but that held even truer for Amish women. "Maybe we have more in common than I thought. It was thoughtful of you to bring them; I appreciate it. I've seen issues of the *Geographic* before. I don't know why I haven't subscribed to it. They're interesting."

"I thought so. I know our *ordnung* teaches us to live apart from the world, but that doesn't mean we should be ignorant of it."

Maybe he'd been hasty in his judgment of Katie Byler, he thought. She wasn't a bad sort, once you got to know her better. He sighed and looked around at the yard and sparkling surface of the pond and took a deep breath of the fresh air. It felt good out here. Small fish were feeding near the surface, and he could just make out some of them jumping.

"You know, if you like to make fishing lures," Katie said. "Maybe we could bring some of your tools into the house. You could work on them at the kitchen table or even in bed. It would give you something to do...to help pass the time."

He nodded. "That might be a good idea. If you wouldn't mind, I can make a list of what I'd need. My workshop is over at the mill."

Katie had found a four-foot stepladder and unfolded it.

"What are you doing?" He'd seen the broom

and thought she meant to sweep the porch, which could certainly use it. He had to admit that the porch was a little cluttered. There was a bucket with scraps for the chickens, a couple of fishing poles, a rake, a folding chair that he'd carried in to mend one rainy day, before he'd had the accident, and a few tools and cardboard boxes. "Why do you need a ladder?"

She used the broom handle to point at a bird's nest along the eaves.

There was a rip in the screen at the far end of the porch that let the swallows in. They'd made nests here in the spring when they were raising babies. Actually, they'd made four nests, two from the previous year. He winced. Had it been two winters ago that a tree branch had fallen and torn the screen? He should have cleaned away the old bird nests. The swallows wouldn't use the old nests next year. They'd build new ones.

"You need to get someone to fix that hole," she pointed out. "You can't keep mosquitoes out without mending that screen."

"Haven't noticed they're bad. Besides, the barn swallows eat the mosquitoes."

"*Ne*, but I'll doubt you spend much time on the porch. And birds belong outside, not in. They make a mess." She looked around the space and sighed. "Not that you'd notice, I suppose." She climbed the ladder, revealing neat ankles and shapely bare feet before he realized he was staring and looked away.

"Are you calling me dirty?" he asked, not really offended. She had very high arches, and she seemed nimble. She certainly wasn't afraid of heights like Susan had been. He'd tried to get her to climb the steps to the top floor of the mill once, and she'd gone white-faced and clingy on him.

Katie used the broom to knock loose one of the swallow nests. "Now don't go all huffy on me, Freeman," she said between whacks. "I can't imagine how one man does all the work it must take to run this mill, even with the help of an apprentice."

"Hired man," he corrected. "I told Shad that I'd make him my apprentice if he showed promise. I'm still waiting."

"It must be a trial, trying to find good help."

He didn't bite on that one.

"What kind of a name is Shad?" she asked. "Sounds English. Is he English?"

"Shad Gingrich? *Ne*, his name is Shadrach. From the Bible. The fiery oven."

"Oh, that Shadrach. I didn't know there were any Gingrichs around here."

"There aren't. Shad's from Ohio. Uncle Jehu is a friend of his grandfather. He boards at a farm down the road. His family wanted Shad to learn the trade and sent him here to me. He's a little young, though."

"How young?"

"Twenty-one."

"I thought you were twenty when you took over the mill here," she pointed out.

"But he's young for his age," Freeman said quickly. "Milling's serious. You can get hurt around the gears if you're not careful. And you can do a lot of damage to the equipment. It's expensive to repair and difficult to replace parts. There aren't many stone mills still in operation in this country. It's a dying art."

"All the more reason for you to have an apprentice, maybe more than one in case one doesn't work out."

"You're quick to give advice on a trade you know nothing of." He looked up at her. "What makes you think I can afford the price of a second hired man?"

"Apprentice. Take on one younger and he won't cost you as much, and he'll be more willing to take advice. And if you could afford to pay my wages, and I'll only be here temporarily, you can use that money to employ another apprentice." She climbed down, swept the fallen nest and the dirt around it into a dustpan before moving her ladder. "Wait," she said. "Is that Shad coming out of the mill?"

Freeman looked where she was pointing. "*Ya*, that's him carrying a fishing pole. Maybe planning on taking a little leisure on my time when he should be working. Shad!" he shouted. "Shad!"

Katie leaned the broom against the house. "You know, I think you'd heal faster if you weren't so out of sorts all the time. And maybe you'd be in a better mood if you could get out to the mill yourself and see what's going on."

"What? You think I can roll the wheelchair down these steps to the backyard?"

She gave him the same look a mother might give a trying child. "What you need is a ramp, and an apprentice who has time to go fishing has time to build a ramp." She started toward the screen door that led to the yard.

"Where are you going?"

"To tell Shad he needs to find the materials to build a ramp."

"You can't do that," he said.

She whipped around. "Can't do what?"

"Give my hired man orders."

"I can't?" She smirked. "Watch me."

He stared after her as she marched across the

yard intent on having her own way. And then, he couldn't contain himself. He saw the humor in it and laughed.

# Chapter Five

By noon the following day, Shad was well on his way to completing a wheelchair ramp from the house to the sidewalk, and Freeman supposed he should have been pleased. But Katie had invited him to join them for the midday meal and afterwards, when the family sat drinking iced tea on the porch, he'd had to watch Shad making calf eyes at Katie and praising her for her cooking. Every time Katie glanced in the boy's direction, Shad flushed to the roots of his hair. Finally, when Shad remarked for the second time on the amazing qualities of her blackberry pie, Freeman lost patience. "Time you were getting back to work, don't you think, Shadrach?"

"Oh, let the boy digest his dinner," Grossmama said. "He's been at it since early this morning."

Katie glanced up from the elaborate cat's cradle pattern Jehu was attempting and smiled at Shad. "And a good job he's making of it, too."

Shad clutched his straw hat and turned strawberry red up to his ears. It was clear to Freeman that he was smitten with Katie. Every time she opened her mouth, he stared at her as if he expected pearls of wisdom to tumble out.

"Should be finished by supper time," Shad boasted. "Or tomorrow morning at the latest. Solid as the Temple of Jerusalem."

"And we know what happened to that," Freeman quipped.

Katie chuckled, and for an instant, Freeman thought she was laughing *at* him rather than *with* him, but when he looked back at her, he saw that her attention was fixed on Uncle Jehu's string and the tangle he'd made of it.

"Maybe not quite right," Uncle Jehu said before adding his own laughter to Katie's. "I think I need a little practice on Grossmama's spinning wheel."

"A little," Katie agreed. "And Freeman's right. I should be getting back to work, too." She glanced at Freeman. "I brought Sara's hair scissors. After I get the dishes cleared away, I could cut your hair for you."

"Got stuff to do of my own." Grossmama looked at Uncle Jehu. "I could use your help, Jehu," she said.

"My help?" His uncle was trying to untangle his string.

"If you can spare the time."

"*Ya*, time's something I've got plenty of," Uncle Jehu said.

The four of them quickly scattered: Shad to resume his hammering, Freeman's grandmother and uncle to do whatever it was she needed doing, and Katie to clean up the kitchen. Freeman sat there on the porch for a few more minutes.

He had to admit that minus the birds' nests and the boxes and all the rest of the clutter, the porch looked a lot better. The floor could do with a fresh coat of paint, and he still had to fix that torn screen, but Katie had scrubbed and swept and scrubbed some more. From somewhere, she'd found a large crockery butter-churn, gray with a blue wheat design, one that hadn't been used in several generations, and planted tarragon, rosemary and lavender in it. The lip of the churn had a big chip out of it, and there was a hairline crack down one side, but it looked handsome standing by the door, and the herbs made the porch smell fine.

He couldn't get to the mill until Shad finished the ramp, but Katie had promised they'd get him there by the next afternoon. It would take a big load off his mind just to make certain everything was all right with the mechanism and the grain stores. He wanted to check on his cats, too. Shad said he was feeding and watering them but he worried that their water wasn't being changed regularly.

People made a habit of dropping unwanted cats and kittens at farms or along rural roads. And he'd always had a soft spot for strays, so much so that his neighbors had brought him any they found. He wasn't sure how many cats he owned now, but he took his responsibility seriously. He provided good veterinary care and nutritious food for them. In return, the cats kept his grain stores free of rodents. He'd explained to Shad how much to feed the cats and to be certain they had fresh water every day, but Shad didn't like them. So how did he know the boy was actually caring for the cats as he should? And if he was feeding them, he certainly wasn't giving them attention, petting them or calling them by name. Some were tamer than others, but Freeman knew every cat as an individual and he was concerned for their welfare.

Shad's hammering made it difficult to think, so Freeman gave up his comfortable spot on the porch and rolled the wheelchair into the kitchen. Katie was at the sink, soap bubbles up to her elbows, scrubbing away at a large pot. "Nearly done there?" he asked.

"Almost." She turned to smile at him. "Last one."

"You can cut my hair if you're set on it. You've run on about it so much that I suppose I'll have to let you trim it up to get you to stop harping on it."

She laughed. "I suppose I have been annoying." She turned the pot upside down on the drain rack and dried her hands on a towel. "I see you shaved yourself this morning."

He rubbed at his chin. He thought he'd done a passable job. He'd gotten the job done with a nick or two. He didn't think it looked half bad. But he could see by the amused expression in her eyes that she had a different opinion.

"I'll need the razor to shave the back of your neck, so I may as well trim up those rough spots on your chin," she offered.

"Doesn't matter much one way or the other."

"It might, if you have company on Sunday. It's visiting Sunday, and it might be nice if we…I mean, if you…invited someone over. You need contact with friends, especially other men."

"That's true," he admitted. "I have a lot of fondness for my grandmother and Uncle Jehu, but it would be good to hear what someone else has to say. Nothing against you, you understand, but you're a woman."

She shrugged. "I am that." She gave him a half smile. "So, it's settled. Your uncle said that he'd be glad to invite whomever you want. And I'll be happy to make some food for your guests and run it over on Saturday. It's always nice to have something to offer them."

"That's decent of you." Today, she was wearing a gray-blue dress. He liked the blue with her yellow hair. It suited her.

"I'll be glad to do it." She went to her basket and found the scissors. "I'd rather not do this in the kitchen," she said. "I've just swept the floor, and it's hard to get up all the little bits of hair."

"Sounds like you've done this before. Cut a man's hair."

She nodded. "I always cut my *dat*'s, and my brothers'. My mother isn't so good at cutting hair." She smiled. "It always ends up crooked."

"How about yours? Do your haircuts end up crooked?"

"Not yet." Her eyes lit with mischief and she opened and closed the scissors rapidly. "But there's always a first time."

He groaned. "Great." He glanced around. "So if not here, where? The back porch?"

"Too noisy with all that hammering," she said. "How about the front porch? It's not screened in, and with that little breeze, most of the stray hair will just blow away." She picked up the scissors, a comb and a towel that lay folded on the counter and walked purposefully toward the hallway that also led to the living room and the front entrance hall.

"What about me?" he called after her. "Aren't you going to push me out there?"

She stopped, turned, and gave him an amused look. "*Ne.* I am not. Like you told me yesterday, your leg is broken, not your arms. You can manage."

This time when he laughed, she laughed with him.

"You should have seen him, Ellie," Katie said as she removed a still-warm egg from one of the row of hens' nests along the back wall of Sara's chicken house. "He talks about not liking to be dependent on others, then he's asking for this and that. He wants iced tea with extra ice, coffee with more milk than coffee, dumplings with extra broth." She shook her head. "It never ends."

Ellie slid her hand under a clucking hen and pulled out two eggs. "He likes the attention, I suppose."

Katie deposited her egg gently in the straw-filled basket. Sara's chicken house was so new that you could still smell the new lumber and the large casement windows were still relatively clean. The floor was ankle-deep with sawdust, and the laying boxes and roosts were painted a lovely shade of gray-blue. Katie had always been fond of chickens; they were such useful birds. She had never seen a henhouse as nice as this one, and she secretly vowed that when she had her own home, she'd have one built that was just as well-designed.

"Is he handsome?"

Katie inspected another nest. There were three eggs here, two large and one small, probably laid by one of the young pullets. "I suppose. But it's a man's character and not his looks that are important."

"So you aren't interested in him?" Ellie asked.

"Of course not. Whatever gave you that idea? I told you, the man is too set in his ways. I only agreed to help out there as a favor."

Ellie was quiet for a minute, then she said, "I was just thinking. Sara is clever. Do you think she might have placed you in Freeman's household because she thought the two of you might make a match?"

Katie made a face. "Sara wouldn't do that, would she?" She thought for a moment and then shook her head. "Doesn't matter. Freeman doesn't think that way about me. I'm not even sure that we could be friends. It seems like everything I say, he has something to say back."

"*Ach*, a shame." Ellie removed two more eggs from the last nest. "Sixteen. That's two more than yesterday. Sara will have eggs to sell soon. Johanna, down the road, has regular egg customers. English. She said she could take any extra we have and sell them for Sara."

Katie took the basket. "Did Sara tell you that I had a letter from Uriah today?"

"From your Kentucky Uriah, personally? Not from his father?"

"*Ya.*"

Ellie pushed open the chicken house door and held it for Katie. "See, you spoke too soon. He *is* interested."

"I don't know." Katie sighed and pulled a letter from her apron pocket. She set the egg basket on the grass. "Listen to what he says and then tell me whether you think he's interested."

Ellie folded her arms and waited expectantly.

"It starts with *Kathryn*. Not *Dear Kathryn*, just *Kathryn*."

"Go on."

"*You are of an age and mind to marry,*" Katie read.

Ellie rolled her eyes. "Romantic."

Katie nodded. "He continues...*I am the*

*same. Sara says that you have been baptized into the Old Order Amish Church and are in good standing with your community. Likewise. I am building a house and need a wife. If you are of a mind, I will send money for a train ticket. Best you come to Kentucky. This is the busy season for my crops and lumber mill. If you are agreeable, write and say when you are coming. I am hard-working, respectable, and not the best with words. We are not strangers because we grew up next door. I remember you were kind. My bishop tells me marriages built on faith and respect are solid ones. If you come we can see if we are a good match. If you decide not, I will pay your way back home without ill will. Your friend, Uriah.*"

Ellie nibbled at her lower lip. "Gets right to details, doesn't he?"

Katie stifled a giggle.

"But you think he's a good person?"

Katie nodded. "He was a gentle boy. Never complaining. Sweet."

Ellie pointed at the letter in Katie's hand. "I'm not sure his sweetness comes across there."

"*Ne*, it wouldn't. In school, he would never speak up, but he got good grades in math and he always included the younger children in games."

"Kind, then." Ellie considered. "So he could be a disaster…or a treasure. Hard to tell."

"Exactly." Katie picked up the basket of eggs and started toward the house. "Which is why I'm trying to decide if I should accept his offer and go to Kentucky and find out."

The mantel clock chimed nine times and Freeman paused and looked at his grandmother. "It's getting late," he said. "Should I end here?"

*"Ne,"* she answered. "Don't stop yet. You're just getting to the exciting part."

"Go on," his uncle urged.

Freeman shifted the large German Bible on his lap and continued reading from *Exodus*, the story of Moses leading the Israelites out of slavery in Egypt. He kept on until he finished the passage and then closed the holy book. "How's my High German?" he asked.

His grandmother nodded. "Better, much better."

"You would make a good preacher," Uncle Jehu said. "You're content to let God's message speak for itself, and aren't tempted to add your own words."

"Don't wish that on me," Freeman said. Being chosen as preacher for a community was a great responsibility that lasted a lifetime. It wasn't one he would ask for. If it came, he would accept, but he'd never felt that he was called to serve the Lord that way. "There are many better shepherds among my neighbors."

His grandmother took the heavy Bible and carried it back into the front room. Freeman cherished the book. It had been passed down to him from his great-grandfather on his father's side, and it was a possession that he valued greatly. "Thank you," he called after his grandmother. "I should be the one doing that."

"And you will," Uncle Jehu said. He rose and went to the sink and came back with a glass of water. "In case you get thirsty in the night."

His grandmother returned. "I see Katie's been busy in there, as well. That girl's a whirlwind for cleaning." She came to the bed and kissed him on the cheek. "You look so much better, Freeman. I've been worried, not so much over the broken bone in your leg, I knew that would heal, but I've been concerned about you. But I can see that your spirits have risen. You're more your old self."

*"Ya,"* Freeman agreed. "I do feel stronger."

She gazed down at him. "Do you think that has anything to do with Katie? It seems to me that she's brought energy to this house. And to you."

"I don't know about all that," he replied, "but she's got enough energy for two women."

His grandmother smiled. "I'll bid you a good night. Sleep well."

Jehu rose. "I'll just walk you to your door, Ivy."

"Walk me to my door?" She uttered a sound of amusement. "It's not fifty feet from the house. Why would I need you to do that?"

"You never know. It's a full moon tonight, and I heard some of the neighbors saying that their livestock seemed uneasy the last few nights. Raymond said something had lifted one of his Muscovy ducks. Nothing left in the yard but feathers. He thought we might have a coyote prowling around. If so, a full moon night's the worst for predators. No sense in taking any chances."

"Jehu, it's barely full dark. And what you'd do about it if a coyote did come up in the yard, I'm not sure."

His uncle held open the kitchen door for all. "All the same, Ivy, I'll rest easier knowing you're safe inside." She shrugged and gave in good-naturedly, and the two left together. As the door closed behind them, Freeman could hear his uncle talking about wanting to go to Dover in the morning.

Freeman lay back against his pillows. It had been a good day, he realized, an excellent day. Truthfully, he hadn't had such a good day in a long time. Was it possible that his grandmother had hit on something when she'd linked Katie to the improvement in his health and spirits?

Was that possible?

## Chapter Six

Katie reined in her horse close to the back door of Freeman's house and called a greeting to Ivy and Jehu on the porch. It was Saturday afternoon, and she'd brought the groceries that they'd asked her to pick up for them at Bylers' Country Store as well as the fried chicken and potato salad that she'd prepared for them for Sunday. Both Sara and Ellie had insisted on sending something as well: coleslaw and a sweet potato pie from Sara, and Ellie's pickled eggs and an applesauce cake. Since no cooking would be done on the Sabbath, everything could be eaten cold.

"There was no need for you to go to the trouble," Jehu insisted as she began to carry the dishes into the kitchen. "But I'm glad you did. My mouth is watering already."

"And I do appreciate you saving me a trip to

the store." Ivy followed them inside. "Did we give you enough money?'

"More than enough," Katie assured them. "I have change for you both." She glanced around the kitchen. Both Freeman and the wheelchair were nowhere in sight. "I see Freeman managed to get himself outside."

*"Ya,"* Ivy replied with a beaming countenance. "Eli and Charley stopped by to see him. Nothing would do but that they all go out to the horseshoe pit. They usually play horseshoes one evening every week in decent weather."

"Pretty warm out there," Uncle Jehu commented. "Might be they're thirsty by now. Would it be too much trouble for you to take them some cool water?" He waved toward the mill. "The horseshoe pit is on the far side of the mill, near the little pond. Just follow the path. You can't miss them."

"Of course I wouldn't mind," Katie answered. "But I don't want to intrude on Freeman and his friends."

"Nonsense." Ivy peeked into one of the paper grocery bags she'd carried in from Katie's buggy. "This is the best week Freeman has had since his injury. You've perked up his spirits more than the doctor's medicine. I know he'd be happy to see you. And I'm sure they'd appreciate the water."

"Throwing horseshoes is hot work," Uncle Jehu added as he removed three pint-size canning jars from the cabinet. "And a drink delivered by a pretty face is always welcome."

"And what makes you think I have a pretty face?" Katie teased, putting things into the refrigerator. "I might have a nose like a sweet potato and whiskers on my chin."

"Ivy told me," he answered. "But it wouldn't matter if you did have a big nose and *no* chin. Beauty comes from inside, and your words and actions show me more than I could ever see when I had my sight."

Katie swallowed, touched by Jehu's opinion of her. "Then," she managed, "you must know that you have a pretty face, too."

"Pretty hairy," Ivy said, and they all chuckled.

"Well, I can do better than water for the men folk," Katie said. "I brought blackberry iced tea. I'll take some of this cake, too."

Once the groceries and food were put away, Katie packed slices of cake, napkins, a quart of the blackberry tea and the jars to be used for glasses in her wicker basket and carried it down the hill. She followed the man-made water-course around the mill to a picnic area. Freeman was sitting in his wheelchair in the shade of a tree, his broken leg elevated by the leg rest. He was laughing and shouting suggestions to the two men throwing horseshoes.

Freeman's two friends stood at the farthest peg, and Katie recognized the taller man from the chair shop in Seven Poplars. Eli was a skilled craftsman and the manager and partial owner of the Amish-run business. Eli saw her, waved and made a throw that clanked as it hit the peg. The other man, shorter and blond-haired, groaned and made a show of throwing his straw hat down beside the peg and pretending that he was going to stomp on it.

She put her basket down on one of the picnic tables near where Freeman sat. "Anyone thirsty?" she called. "I brought some black-berry tea and cake."

"Katie." Freeman's smiled widened as his friends walked toward them. "This is Katie Byler, the girl I told you was helping out while I'm laid up," he explained. "Katie, this is Eli and Charley. He's a Byler, too. Are you two cousins by any chance?"

*"Ne,"* Katie replied. "Not that I know of."

"Lots of Bylers," Charley agreed. "Glad to know you, Katie, even if we aren't cousins." He beat the sand off his hat on his trouser leg and replaced it on his head. "And I'd like some of that tea. Eli's been feeding me dust this afternoon."

Eli, a nice-looking dark-haired man about

Freeman's age, walked up behind Charley to join them. "How's that chair working out for you?" he asked Katie. "Her brother broke a kitchen chair and she ordered a new one from the shop," he said. "Oak, wasn't it?" he asked Katie.

"It was." She poured the first jar of tea and handed it to Charley. "And so far my brothers haven't got the best of it."

Charley looked from Freeman to Katie. "Been some job, hasn't it?" he teased. "Cleaning a path through Freeman's kitchen?"

Seeing that Freeman was smiling, she smiled, too. "It wasn't that bad."

"This is fine tea, Katie." Charley took a gulp. "I appreciate it."

"You're welcome," she answered, handing Eli and then Freeman jars of the blackberry tea. "But don't let me interfere in your game. I was just on my way home."

"*Ne*, don't go yet," Freeman protested, good-naturedly. "Stay a while. I need you to help me keep an eye on Charley. He cheats if you don't watch him close." He motioned toward a tree stump beside his wheelchair. "Sit here with me."

"I'm not a cheat!" Charley retorted, then grinned. "And if I did nudge my horseshoe an inch closer to the peg, it would be because

I learned the trick from Freeman when we were kids." He drained his glass in four gulps. *"Goot!"* he pronounced. "Really taste those blackberries. I'll have to tell my Miriam to make some." He wiped his mouth with the back of his hand and set the jar on the picnic table. "I thank you for the drink, but I want you to know that Freeman is only making fun. I really don't *need* to cheat to beat him at horseshoes."

Freeman groaned. "Listen to you. How long has it been since you beat me? Months. Tell her, Eli."

Eli offered a slow smile that lit his eyes. "Let's finish this game and I'll give you my opinion on who's a good player and who's not." He downed his drink and walked back to the horseshoe pit. "Winner plays Freeman," he called.

"I wish," Freeman replied. "I'd be doing well to balance on one foot without trying to toss a shoe in the right direction."

"Maybe he could throw from the wheelchair," Katie suggested.

Freeman frowned. "I doubt that's possible."

"Of course you could do it," Katie encouraged. "You could try, at least. You never know. You might be a better horseshoe thrower sitting down than standing."

"Easy for you to say." Freeman glanced at

her sideways. "But I'd be the one looking like a fool."

"She's right," Charley said. "Good idea, Katie. We'll even spot him half the distance. What more could he ask for?"

"Who's saying that you'll be playing Freeman?" Eli called. "The last time I counted, I was ahead."

"Just warming up," Charley answered.

Katie laughed as the men resumed their game. When she glanced back at Freeman, she found him studying her. Self-conscious, she turned away and saw a boy in his early teens accompanied by a much smaller child, walking down from the mill. The boys were carrying cane fishing poles and the older one had a tin can, presumably bait, she thought. "Looks like you have some fishermen," she said, gesturing toward the newcomers.

"The King boys." Freeman waved, and the young people waved back. "I let the neighbor kids fish down here. It's safer than the big pond because the banks aren't as steep and the water is much shallower here. Good for little kids. Lots of sunfish and a few nice-sized catfish." He raised an eyebrow. "The water's too warm and not deep enough for the big bass."

"You seem to know a lot about fishing."

"Not as much as I'd like to." He offered a hint

of a smile. "The bass still outsmart me most of the time. Grossmama says it's good for my character. She thinks I show a lack of humility as it is."

Katie laughed.

He cocked his head. "That mean you agree with her?"

She shrugged.

"Still," she said, "it's kind of you to give the children a place to fish." Charley yelped with pleasure, and she glanced back toward the horseshoe players to see that he'd made a ringer. "I like your friends."

"I've known them for years. They're good men."

*And I think you are, too*, Katie mused as she watched Freeman finish a slice of the cake and toss the crumbs to a mother mallard and her ducklings that paddled over to beg for scraps. The baby ducklings were adorable, small bobbing balls of feathers with black eyes. They couldn't have been much more than a week or two old. "It's nice here," she observed with a contented sigh. "Peaceful."

Charley groaned as Eli won the round.

"In spite of Charley?" Freeman teased.

*"Ya,"* she answered. "In spite of Charley." She turned her attention to the little boy on the edge of the pond who was concentrating on his

fishing line with the cork bobber. The child was as cute as the ducklings. He wore dark trousers, a straw hat and a green shirt identical to his older brother. Both boys were barefoot and had the same light brown hair, blue eyes and freckled snub noses. "They look so much alike, they must be brothers," she said, indicating the youthful fishermen.

"They are," Freeman said.

Katie's gaze lingered on the smallest boy. She could imagine having a son like that of her own some day. Seeing him reminded her that having children, having a family of her own, was her main reason for considering Uriah's offer.

"Freeman!" Eli called. "You're up. Roll yourself over here and prepare for a whipping."

"Go on," Katie urged. "Try it, at least. You can't do any worse than Charley."

"Thanks a lot," Charley said. But his easy grin told her that he'd taken no offense at her teasing.

"Maybe Katie would like to show us how the game is played." Freeman threw her a challenging look.

"You think I couldn't?" she flung back playfully.

"Come on, Katie," Charley dared. "Start him off. Throw just one set for Freeman."

Freeman glanced at Charley. "Don't encourage her."

Katie put down the jars she'd been gathering and walked over to the peg. She reached down and picked up a horseshoe. "Are you certain you want me to throw this? I might show the three of you up."

Eli stepped back to give her room. "We'll take the risk. Go ahead. Throw."

"For who?" she asked. "You or Freeman?"

"By all means, start off for me," Freeman called. "Start me off with a ringer."

Katie turned the heavy horseshoe in her hand, gauging the weight.

"Come one, Katie. You can do it!" Freeman encouraged.

Here goes nothing, she thought. She sighted the far peg, took a long stride and let the horseshoe fly out of her grasp exactly the way her father had taught her. And then, unconsciously, she shut her eyes. She gritted her teeth, prepared for the men's laughter, but instead, what she heard was the solid metal clunk of her horseshoe striking the peg.

"Ringer!" Charley yelled.

"Good throw," Eli pronounced.

"Look at that!" Charley yelped with excitement. "A ringer. First try."

Opening her eyes, she turned to Freeman and

threw him a triumphant look. His face showed his obvious surprise…and something else she couldn't quite put her finger on. "I played with my brothers," she explained, suddenly feeling embarrassed, with no idea why. She walked toward him. "Every Saturday. And they never spotted me any distance. Not since I was eleven years old."

Freeman didn't say anything, only nodded, but he kept watching her. Studying her.

Katie gathered up the empty jars the men had drunk from, feeling flushed and slightly uncomfortable. Why did Freeman keep looking at her?

"Thank you for the tea and the cake," Eli said. "I appreciate it."

"We all appreciate it," Charley added. "And, Katie, you can play doubles with me anytime."

As Katie turned to walk away, Freeman spoke loud enough for only her to hear him. "I never expected that. Not in a hundred years, Katie." His voice was surprisingly gentle and filled with… What was that? *Admiration?*

Katie mumbled something about seeing him Monday and walked briskly up the hill, carrying her basket. Halfway to her buggy, her heart was still beating too fast. What was wrong with her? she wondered. And then it occurred to her why she was feeling this way…happy and scared at the same time. Hot and cold. Bold and shy.

She stopped in midstride, taking her basket in her arms and clutching it tightly. She had to be mistaken. It couldn't be true.

She couldn't possibly *like* Freeman.

# Chapter Seven

Freeman stretched his good leg and shifted his weight to find a more comfortable position in the wheelchair. They'd finished the noon meal more than an hour earlier, and the porch with its faint breeze off the millpond was a cool retreat from the midsummer sun. Katie had returned to her task of pulling weeds in the flowerbed by the steps after clearing away the dinner dishes, and he'd been just sitting here watching her. He was surprisingly in a good mood. It was nice, after the quiet weekend, having Katie back at the house again with all her chatter and giving orders, so nice that he couldn't think of much to complain about.

"Finding any flowers in there?" he called to her. "Or just weeds?"

"Plenty of flowers." Katie tossed another handful of chickweed into the wheelbarrow.

"Grossmama said she had perennials in there, but I couldn't see them," Freeman said. "I was meaning to try and clean them up for her, but I had so much to do at the mill, I just didn't get to it."

"I can see that," Katie replied. She'd come prepared for outdoor work today. Her apron was a sturdy one, her blue dress faded from much use and many washings, and her pinned-up hair covered with a denim-blue scarf instead of her usual *kapp*. The blue of her dress made her eyes seem even bluer. He wondered how it was that he hadn't noticed how large her eyes were and how they didn't seem to miss a thing.

"So Ivy asked you to do some weeding for her?" Katie said.

"A while back." He shrugged. "But I've been really busy. Did you have a good visiting Sunday?" he asked in an attempt to steer the conversation away from his failings in the yard maintenance department. His Sunday had been somewhat of a disappointment. They were supposed to have company, as Katie had suggested, but that fell through. An illness in the family. So there'd been no one here to talk to but his grandmother and Uncle Jehu, and they'd spent so much time together recently that they'd already heard all of each others' stories and opinions. He'd enjoyed seeing Eli and Charley on Saturday, and the next day had been a bit of a letdown after the fun he'd had with them. And, he had to admit, with Katie. Seeing her in a social capacity had been surprising, but in a good way. His buddies would be talking for a long time about the ringer that Katie had made.

"It was nice," Katie said. "Sara had a bunch of company. Rebecca and her husband came by with their family, and brought home-made peach ice cream. And there were…other people."

Freeman smiled. "Sounds as if I missed something good."

"You did. Sara and Ellie made lemon pound cake on Saturday, and it was nice to have the peach ice cream to serve with the cake to guests."

The cake and ice cream sounded like something he would have enjoyed. Why hadn't she thought to bring him a slice of cake? He was especially fond of lemon pound cake, so much so that he could almost taste it. "Must be pretty lively living at Sara's," Freeman observed. "Always somebody coming by."

"I like it. It's not home, of course, but Sara makes me feel as if it is."

"You said *other people.* Who else came to visit?" he asked.

She hesitated. "There was LeRoy, a cousin of

someone. Guengerich, I think Sara said his last name was. Up visiting relatives from western Virginia. She said that he wanted to meet me."

"One of Sara's clients?" Freeman frowned. He didn't know any Geungerichs from Virginia, but he could picture the man in his imagination—tall, rangy, hat brim a little too wide, and beady eyes too close together. Freeman seemed to recall that someone had told him that those members of ultra-conservative churches in the mountains wore only a single suspender on their trousers. Two suspenders were deemed too fancy. He wondered if this LeRoy fit the image. "Is he in the market for a wife?"

Katie glanced up at him and shrugged. She had stopped weeding. "Doesn't matter if he is or isn't. We didn't hit it off. He asked me to go for a walk with him, but we didn't have much to talk about. Mostly he went on about the mildew in his garden. I don't think I responded the way he wanted me to. He lost interest pretty quickly after I told him he should make a spray from baking soda and dish soap and treat it with that."

"What makes you think he wasn't interested in you?" Freeman straightened up, liking the tale better now that it was clear that this Virginia stranger hadn't taken Katie's fancy.

"Because when he left Sara's after the ice

cream and cake, he went home to take supper with Jane Stutzman."

"Jane? I know her. Pretty girl."

"*Ya*, she is. I'm sure LeRoy thought so."

"But if he wasn't to your liking, what difference does it make who he had supper with?"

She stood up and brushed the dirt off her skirt. "It doesn't. I'm not really seeking a match, anyway. I'm already spoken for—sort of. I'm seriously considering the suit of an old neighbor of mine. Uriah. And he's already said that he is willing to marry me."

"Old, huh?" Freeman frowned. "How old? Old enough to be your father? Your grandfather?"

Katie laughed. "*Ne*. Nothing like that. Uriah's my age. I just meant that we grew up next door to each other. Did you think I was planning on marrying a graybeard?"

He considered. "It happens. Lots of girls marry older men, especially girls who have a hard time in the marriage market."

Her eyebrows went up and he could tell her dander was ruffled. "You think I'm having a *hard time*?"

He shrugged. "No offense, but Sara, well, we all know that she specializes in hard-to-place cases."

"And?"

Freeman couldn't tell by the expression on Katie's face now whether she was annoyed or intrigued by the way this conversation was going. "You *are* living with the matchmaker."

"So you think that means I'm one of Sara's hard-to-place matches?"

"I didn't say that." He rolled the wheelchair closer to the open screen door. "It's just that Sara has a reputation for being the best at what she does. I'm surprised that she'd introduce you to this LeRoy and then he'd run off to Jane Stutzman's and leave you standing there. Doesn't sound like the type of man Sara should be trying to fix you up with. The whole idea of a matchmaker is to find someone suitable for you. Obviously LeRoy wasn't someone who would be suitable."

Katie folded her arms and got a stubborn look on her face. There was a little bit of dirt on her chin, and he thought about mentioning it to her, but it seemed as though she was already on edge, so he didn't. "So you have something against matchmakers? Or is it Sara you doubt?"

"I like Sara well enough."

"So it's the whole matchmaker thing?"

Freeman shrugged.

"Funny you should think that."

"And why is that?"

She fixed him with a stare that could have

burned through steel. "It just strikes me as odd, you having so many opinions on me finding a husband when you're older than I am and have no wife. Surely the church elders have mentioned it to you. Most men your age have a family already."

"I'll marry when the time is right," he answered brusquely. "I have a lot of responsibility with the mill and—"

"Sound like excuses to me." She came up the steps to the porch and he had to roll back to make way for her. "With men," she went on, "it should be easy. You are the ones who do the asking. Women have to wait for someone to notice them."

"And go to matchmakers, apparently."

"Some do," she agreed. "I think it's better to consider someone like Sara who's made dozens of matches—maybe even hundreds. And not one of her couples has ever failed. Can you believe that? Every marriage arrangement she made has been a success. Look what she did for Addy and Gideon Esch. Have you been to the new butcher shop?"

Freeman nodded.

"Everyone thought that Addy would stay home with her mother until her hair turned gray, but Sara found her a husband. And they're happy. Sara says that they'll be welcoming a little dishwasher or sausage maker into their family by winter."

"Theirs does seem like a good match," he agreed. "And from what I hear, Gideon's parents were in despair of his finding a wife. So, it seems that Sara—"

"Knew what she was doing when she brought them together," Katie finished, cutting him off. "Like I said. She's good at what she does." Her expression changed, becoming suddenly vulnerable. "But it doesn't seem to be working for me. Not unless you count Uriah, and his family contacted Sara, not him. It was my brother Isaac who suggested we let Sara handle the negotiations."

He gave a doubtful grunt. "Negotiations? Sounds like Uriah is buying a sheep. How long has it been since the two of you have seen each other? Exchanged words?"

"A year. Maybe a little longer. But it's not as though he's a stranger," she added quickly. "And we know the family well. They're good people, well thought of by their church community."

He rolled back to make room for her. "You've never met anyone here in Kent County you wanted to marry? None of the boys you grew up with? Walked out with?" he added.

"*Ne.* I've ridden home from singings with

boys a couple of times, but no one has ever wanted to walk out with me. Sometimes, I wonder if there's something wrong with me. I see younger girls courting, marrying. Even having their first child. And I'm still living with my mother and brother. And now his wife." Her eyes grew large and wistful as she sat down on the edge of a chair. "So I have a lot of faith in Sara and her wisdom, maybe not so much in myself when it comes to finding the right man."

He lowered his cast to the floor, leaned forward, and lowered his voice. "Are you asking my opinion?"

She looked up suddenly. "Your opinion? On what?"

"You know. Your…trouble. Dating."

She drew herself up, the apples of her cheeks growing rosy. "Certainly not. I'm just explaining to you why Sara—"

"Well, since you asked," he said, interrupting. "My guess is that you're a little too outspoken for a woman. Too quick to give your opinion on things."

"What do you mean by that?" She rose and began to pace the length of the porch. "Do you think I should be like Jane? Say, '*Ya*, LeRoy,' and never have a thought of my own?"

"I didn't say that. I *said*, that in my estimation, you have too many opinions. You never hold back from giving them, asked for or not."

"Why shouldn't I speak my mind?" she demanded, spinning around to come toward him. "You do. You've got opinions on how scrapple should be cooked, how much milk goes in coffee even when it's not yours," she sputtered. "Men give opinions all the time."

"But you're not a man. You're a young woman. Hasn't someone ever told you that you should show more…more…" He hesitated, searching for the right word.

She stopped in front of him and waved away his argument with a quick gesture. "Maybe it's in my nature, or maybe because I grew up in a household with brothers, but I've never wasted time with mealy-mouth pretense. I'm a sensible woman with just as good a mind as you or any other man. If I think something, I say it."

"That might do among the Englishers, but the bishops tell us that a woman's place is—"

"I know what the Bible says." She dropped her hands to her hips. "If I had a husband, I would show him the respect due—"

"But you have no husband." He shrugged. "Maybe your headstrong attitude is the reason. You have a face and form to attract any man with eyes in his head, but your manner—"

"You approve of my face, then?" She cocked her head to one side.

"I'm sorry." He felt his face grow warm. "I shouldn't have said that."

She studied him, seeming to consider if he was being truthful. "You think I'm pretty? Is that what you're giving your opinion on now? My looks?"

"Katie Byler. You are the most outrageous…" For seconds, it seemed to him that his enjoyable afternoon was fast sliding into chaos. And then he shook his head and chuckled. "You're never boring. I'll say that for you."

Katie didn't take that as the compliment he meant it to be. She pointed at him. "Back to what you were saying. So, you approve of my being pretty so long as I mind my tongue and don't speak my mind?"

"I didn't say that. You asked me why you weren't attracting more suitors and I—"

"I did *not* ask you that," she exclaimed. "You took it upon yourself to give your view on a matter that I consider none of your affair." She headed back down the porch steps. "I think it's time we ended this conversation before one of us says something that we can't take back." She pointed toward the kitchen. "There are leftovers in the refrigerator. I'm going back to Sara's, where I won't offend anyone with my outrageous behavior."

"But it's early," he said, immediately contrite. He didn't want her to go. The best part of his day was when she was here...even when she was giving her opinions. "You never leave this early. I was hoping that I could have a little more iced tea before—"

"You know where it is," she said, charging down the sidewalk, barefoot. "You're capable of fetching your own tea."

"Wait. If you're bound on going, I'll have Shad hitch up your buggy and—"

She raised her hand. "No need. I can do it myself. A handy skill if I'm going to be left an old maid." With that, she turned her back on him, and hurried off, her back stiff, her movements quick and sharp.

Freeman stared after her, not certain what had gone wrong. All he'd done was give her his honest opinion.

Now she was angry with him.

Thunder rumbled in the distance as Katie hurried to Sara's clothesline. When she'd left Freeman's house, barefoot and without her basket, the sun had been shining. By the time she turned the horse into Sara's lane half an hour later, dark clouds were scudding overhead and the sky in the west was fast darkening.

Katie jerked a bath towel from the line so hard that two clothespins catapulted into the air. Mumbling under her breath, she shook out the towel, folded it quickly and tossed it into a laundry basket in the grass. Try as she might, she couldn't get Freeman's advice out of her head. She was annoyed… and his know-it-all attitude had ruined what had been a lovely day for her.

And to think… Saturday she'd actually thought she might be falling for him. She felt as if steam might come out of her ears.

What made Freeman Kemp think that he had the right to criticize her? she fumed. And not only her. He'd insinuated that Sara didn't know what she was doing. Not to mention the unkind things he'd hinted at about Uriah, a man he'd never met. What had ever caused her to have such a high opinion of Freeman, she didn't know. No wonder he was well on his way to being an old bachelor. She yanked a dishtowel off the clothesline, sending another pin flying.

"Whoa. What has the laundry done to you today?" Sara began to gather the fallen clothespins. "A bad day?"

*"Ach."* Katie shook her head. "I'm sorry.

I didn't mean to..." She sighed and let her thought go unexpressed.

Sara dropped the clothespins into their bag and reached for the top corner of a sheet. "I don't know who got on your bad side but I wouldn't want to be that person."

Together, Katie and Sara removed and folded the sheet neatly.

"Forgive me." Katie exhaled. "I'm just in a sour mood."

Sara moved along the clothesline with efficiency. "What went wrong at Freeman's?"

Katie felt the steam rising again. "That man."

"What?" Sara asked. "You came home Saturday all smiles and talk of him. I thought you liked him."

"I did." Then Katie quickly corrected herself. "I mean, I *do* like him—as an employer. But..."

Sara's dark eyes twinkled as she reached for a white pillowcase snapping in the wind. "But...he said something to set you off."

"Yes. No. He's just..." She searched for the right words, ones that might not sound judgmental. "So sure of himself."

"About?"

"You name it."

"Anything in particular?" Sara pressed.

Katie leaned over the clothesline. "He took

it upon himself to give me advice about finding a husband."

"Oh, my." Sara's bonnet strings fluttered in the breeze.

"It's none of his affair," Katie said.

"I'd heard that Freeman was outspoken," Sara replied. She tucked several clothespins in her mouth and began to snatch washcloths off the line.

The first drops of rain spattered on Katie's cheeks. "Oh, no!" she cried, and she hurried to get the clothes down before rain drenched them. Grabbing the last towels, Katie added them to the laundry basket, picked it up and ran for the open carriage shed with Sara two steps behind.

Laughing, they ducked into the shelter seconds before the first wave of rain hit the roof of the outbuilding. "That was a close one," Sara said.

Katie nodded. It was a three-bay shed containing Sara's buggy and small pony cart, her own buggy, and racks for holding the harnesses and cleaning supplies. The space smelled of leather and the peeled cedar crossbeams that formed the structure of the roof. Katie had always been fond of carriage sheds. For Amish children, they were a favorite spot to play in all seasons, cool and shady in summer and out of the wind and weather in winter.

"I'm sorry for being so contrary," Katie said after a moment.

"*Ne.* I have always believed in heeding your feelings. Keep them bottled up inside and eventually they explode."

"But I didn't need to take my temper out on the wash," Katie allowed.

Sara shrugged. "Why not? You can't hurt a towel's feelings. And clothespins are made of wood. What can they expect but to end up as kindling?" She sat on a wagon seat that her hired help, Hiram, used when he cleaned and oiled the harness. She motioned for Katie to sit beside her.

Lightning struck a dead tree across the pasture and Katie blinked at the flash and loud crack. Rain sheeted down the roof and formed a curtain at the front of the shed. "I think we got the wash in just in time," she mused.

"You think?" Sara laughed. She pulled her legs up and wrapped her arms around them as a child might do. She was barefoot, her skin tanned to a honey-brown, her small, sturdy feet high-arched. "You're not afraid of storms, are you?"

Katie shook her head.

"Me, neither." Sara stared out the open doorway. "In fact, I've always liked them. Of course, I don't care to be outside when there's lightning nearby. I'm not so foolish. But this is nice, hearing the rain on the roof, and knowing how much the garden and the farmers' crops will love the water."

"It is a good sound," Katie agreed. With the arrival of the storm, her anxiety had passed. Freeman's words no longer had as much power to affect her as they had. Maybe because now that she'd calmed down a little, she knew in her heart of hearts that he hadn't meant to be unkind to her. It was just his way. Maybe a little bit like her own way, sometimes.

"Rain always eases the heat." Katie glanced sideways at Sara, thinking how wise and calm the older woman seemed. Without realizing that she was going to share what had happened with Sara, she found herself repeating the conversation between her and Freeman that had upset her so.

"It sounds as though he meant well," Sara offered. Mischief gleamed in her expression. "But men rarely understand very much about women and the way they will accept well-meaning, if poorly expressed, advice."

"He's a fine one to tell me how to find a husband when he's obviously had no luck finding a wife," Katie declared.

"But do you think he was trying to be unpleasant in saying those things?" Sara asked.

"*Ne*, but—"

"Then he said them either as a friend or as an interested party."

Katie looked at Sara and blinked. "What do you mean, *interested party*?"

Sara shrugged. "Maybe that's not right. It's probably that he is genuinely concerned. You've been a big help to him and his family. I'm sure that he means well."

Katie didn't say anything.

"And maybe…" Sara fixed her with a compelling gaze. "There's some merit in what the man said."

Katie was taken aback. "You're not taking Freeman's side?"

Sara laced her fingers together. "Personally, I like outspoken women. I've often been accused of speaking my mind, as well. But I'm not in the market for a husband. It might be that once you stop smarting from the supposed insult, you'll give some thought about the good sense of what he said."

"So I should simper and stare at the ground and say, '*Ya*, Freeman. Whatever you think, Freeman'?"

"Only if you want him to take you for a very silly girl," Sara told her, laughing. She stood. "The rain is letting up. You can bring the clothes in with you when you come." She smiled at her. "Just think about it, Katie. And ask yourself why a man like Freeman would take such an interest in a female friend's affairs." Sara removed her apron and pulled it over her head and dashed out of the shed, walking swiftly toward the house.

Katie followed a few steps until she stood at the edge of the shed. Drops of water were still sliding off the roof and they splashed cool and clean across her face. What had Sara meant by that, she wondered. Could it be that Freeman was right and she was wrong? Or was it more than that? Why did Freeman care about her finding a husband?

## Chapter Eight

Katie squeezed the sponge, letting the excess soapy water fall back into the pail before turning again to the dirty windowsill, which she attacked with glee. She couldn't guess when Freeman's parlor woodwork had last been scrubbed, and it gave her a fierce satisfaction to clean away every trace of dust and cobwebs so that the room would be fit to host church Sundays once he'd fully recovered from his accident. It was a lovely front room, or it would be when she finished with it.

There were two windows on the front and a fireplace and another window on the west wall. The fireplace had been closed up and a cast-iron stove added for heating, but the original mantel still remained, as well as the original hardwood floor. The dwelling had been built in the early nineteenth century as a simple farmhouse and it retained much of the original plastered walls and handcrafted wainscoting. Once the windows were washed, the room would be clean and bright and perfect for prayer and contemplating the glory of God.

Thunderstorms had passed in the night, leaving the morning cool and refreshing; it would be a nice day to work outside. If she got all the woodwork in here scrubbed before it was time to begin the noon meal, she might have time to start painting the porch outside this afternoon. Ivy had assured her that there was unopened white paint in the cellar that had been purchased for the front and back porch. As with weeding the flowerbeds, Freeman had had good intentions, but hadn't gotten to the actual painting.

The thought of him made her smile.

Freeman had been unusually pleasant at breakfast, praising the crispiness of her scrapple and taking a second helping of her *pfannkuchen* served with Sara's homemade blueberry syrup. She'd half expected him to be cross after their exchange the previous afternoon and her leaving early in a huff, but he made no mention of it, and she was content to let ruffled feathers lie.

She eyed the smudgy windowpanes that were six over six. They would be next, both inside and out. She'd seen ammonia under the kitchen sink, and used copies of the *Budget* would do to shine the glass to a fare-thee-well. She'd scrub this room from top to bottom and bring in flowers from Ivy's garden so that the spacious chamber would glow with welcome. It was a fine old house that Freeman had inherited from his parents, and if he ever found a bride to please him, she'd not have cause to complain that a careless housekeeper had left it untidy.

She dipped her sponge again into the soapy water and, hearing a sound behind her, turned to see Freeman in the doorway. He was in his wheelchair, attempting to maneuver his outstretched leg through the opening.

"I can't find the scissors. The large ones with the black handles," he said. "Do you know where they are?"

"In the big drawer below the window, just to the left of the sink," she answered as she squeezed the excess water from the sponge. "Where they belong, and where you should be sure to put them when you're done with them."

His eyebrows went up. "You think I need to be told to put away my own scissors?"

She nodded. "If you put them back in the same place every time, you'll always know where to find them. Can't find them if one day they're left here, the next there." She gestured with the sponge.

He gave her a rueful look. "They are *my* scissors. I think I'm free to put them where I like."

She shrugged. "*Ya*, but of no use to you if you can't find them."

"I'll have you know that I organize all my tools and know exactly where they are."

She beamed at him. "An excellent practice." She hesitated. "Can you think of somewhere you'd rather keep the kitchen scissors than the kitchen drawer? On the porch, maybe?"

"*Ne.* They'd soon rust out there. The big drawer is fine."

"Good. We agree." She shook the damp sponge at him to emphasize her instruction. "All I'm saying is, remember to put them back. I found them under your hospital bed yesterday, and last week they were on the porch." She turned back to the windowsill and began to scrub it again. It was time that they moved the bed out of the kitchen. If he could get himself in and out of the wheelchair, there was no reason his bed couldn't go in the empty downstairs bedroom. The kitchen would be easier to maintain without his bed taking up a large portion of it.

There was no sound indicating the departure of the wheelchair. Katie glanced over her shoulder. "Something else you need?"

Freeman straightened his shoulders and an odd, almost embarrassed expression flickered over his handsome face. "Katie?"

*"Ya?"* She lowered her sponge and gave him her full attention.

He took a deep breath. "I hope…that is… I…" His forehead creased and he stopped and then started again. "I wanted to ask you. Did I hurt your feelings yesterday, saying what I did about you being outspoken?"

*"Ne.* What would make you think that?" She didn't meet his gaze, but she could feel her cheeks flush.

"You seemed…well…you left in a rush. Early. And you left your shoes."

Now she felt a little silly. "I did finish early. I needed to get home ahead of the storm," she said quickly, which was true, after a fashion, and not exactly a fabrication. She decided to ignore the subject of her shoes. "And a good thing that I did. Lightning struck a tree—"

"On the road when you were driving back to Sara's?" He rolled the wheelchair a little farther into the room.

She shook her head, feeling foolish that she'd made something of nothing in an effort to cover her own discomfort. "*Ne*. After I got home. It was just a dead tree in the neighbor's field."

"Lightning can be dangerous. I knew it to strike a man's horse once, while he was driving. The animal was never the same. Never safe to trust in harness again."

She dropped her sponge in the bucket and took a few steps toward Freeman. "I was in no danger," she admitted. "And my horse was already safe in Sara's barn."

"Good." He struck the armrest of the chair with the flat of his hand to emphasize his words. "I'd feel responsible if you came to harm on the way home from the mill."

She smiled, touched by his genuine concern for her welfare. "It would hardly be your fault," she said lightly. "You have no control over the weather."

"I guess not, but I'd feel responsible just the same."

"But I'm clearly not hurt."

He chuckled. "Or the horse."

She smiled again and nodded agreement. "Or the horse, thanks be to God."

"Amen to that."

He smiled back at her, and before she could think better of it, she asked, "What kind of things? Specifically."

"I'm sorry?" he answered.

She wondered if it was mistake, going down this path, but it was too late. And maybe she really did care what he thought. "Yesterday. When you said I was too outspoken. What did you mean? What sort of things do I say that make me outspoken?"

Freeman pressed his lips together in a thin line and tugged at the lobe of one ear. "Are you sure you want to hear this? It's just my opinion."

She nodded. "*Ya*, I want to know." She shrugged. "Being myself doesn't seem to be working. Maybe a man's perspective could be…" Not just any man's, she thought. Freeman's perspective, because increasingly, what he thought mattered to her. "Maybe you could tell me," she suggested. "Point out what I say or do that's offensive, when I do it."

He ran a hand through his hair. He wasn't wearing a hat, and it struck her how nice his hair looked now that she'd cut it and he'd washed it. There were little highlights of auburn that shimmered when he moved his head. His hair had felt soft and smelled good. She could remember the smooth texture as it had slipped through her fingers. Cutting Freeman's hair had been nothing like cutting her brothers' hair and she wondered if it had been immodest of her to initiate such an intimate task.

"I didn't say you were offensive."

She just stood there looking at him.

"I don't want to hurt your feelings," he said huskily.

She crossed her arms, waiting.

He exhaled, knowing he wasn't going to get out of this. "It's not always *what* you say," he told her slowly. "So much as *the way* you say it."

She swallowed, her mouth dry. "I don't understand. Give me an example."

He hesitated. "It's…well…like you just did. About the scissors."

She stiffened, feeling suddenly self-conscious. "You were offended because I asked you to put them back when you were finished with them? If you already knew to do it, you wouldn't have had to come to me asking where they were."

"And there's that, too. That's what I mean." He pointed at her. "I'll tell you what raises a man's hackles. It's not about right or wrong. It's your tone. It comes out sounding as if you're giving orders to a child."

"But that wasn't my intention." Now she was upset that he had taken her words all wrong. "Truly, all I was doing was stating the truth. I certainly don't consider you a child. It's just that in my experience, men…most men never remember to put household items back where they belong. They simply leave them lying where they've last used them."

"But I don't do that," he defended. "At least I don't think I do."

"Someone did," she reminded him. "Twice the scissors were left out this week."

He looked down, exhaled and looked up at her again. "Point taken. But when you brought up the scissors, you didn't politely ask me to put them back where I'd found them. You *told* me where I should put them when I was done. And you were quick to point out the previous error of my ways."

Katie thought for a moment and then grimaced. "When you put it like that, I can see what you mean. It didn't come out as I intended. I was joking." She met his gaze. "Sort of."

"Then you should have made it clear that you were teasing. A smile would have helped. A softer tone, maybe." He exhaled as if considering his next words. "Katie, the truth is that… you can be intimidating."

"Me?" She touched her collarbone, in genuine surprise. "Intimidating? To a man?"

"*Particularly* to a man."

"Okay." She gritted her teeth. "Maybe I am a little overbearing at times. I'll give you that. But if you knew my brothers and how they—"

"Sorry, Katie. No excuse. I'm not your brother, and neither is any young man you might want to walk out with. And I...or *he* would rather not be chastised by a pretty girl he's interested in. The minute a man hears a woman talking like that, he begins to imagine what it will sound like in twenty years. Truth be told, it scares us."

What registered first was that he'd referred to her as a pretty girl again, and the second was that when she'd told Sara what had happened, Sara had said nearly the same thing.

She felt herself smiling again. She couldn't help it. *Freeman thought she was pretty.* She met his gaze again and realized he was waiting for her to say something. "So...you think it something so simple that's keeping me from finding a beau?" she ventured, her voice sounding low and husky. *He thought she was pretty.* "I never supposed that speaking directly was such an affront to men."

He settled back in his chair and folded his arms over his freshly ironed blue shirt. It was short-sleeved and looked ever so much better since she'd mended the tear on the left shoulder seam and sewn the loose button back on. In her mind he looked more like a successful mill owner and not so much like the hired hand. *And he thought she was pretty.*

"Some men are more easily offended than others," he explained. "And some are drawn to mealy-mouthed women who have no opinions. I think you can find a happy medium between being yourself, Katie, and being a shrew."

She arched one eyebrow. "A shrew?"

He made a comical grimace. "Very near. Sometimes."

"I never meant that." She nibbled on her lower lip. Did she really come off sounding like a *shrew*? "I need to work on this, don't I?"

"Afraid so." He held her gaze for a moment and then lifted his shoulder and let it fall. "If you want, I could give you some pointers. If I hear you say something that's…could be said differently, I'll tell you."

She considered his offer. She *did* want to marry; she wanted children and a home of her own. And for an instant she imagined herself mistress of not just any house but *this* one. After all, he did think she was pretty. And even though they had a rough start, they did seem to get along well, now that they knew each other a little better. "So you'll tell me if I step over the line?"

He nodded. "As gently as I can."

He smiled at her and she smiled back. And they both just kept smiling at each other. It should have been an awkward moment, but it wasn't. She liked the feeling it gave her, him looking at her that way.

Finally, she glanced back at her bucket. "I suppose I should finish up this window."

*"Ya,"* he agreed. "There's a stack of paperwork waiting for me over at the mill. Computer stuff. Billing. Tax records. My head is clearer now that the pain has eased off my leg. I was thinking I could do a little work. I've fallen behind since the accident."

Katie tucked a wisp of hair behind her ear. "Couldn't it wait until afternoon? I could take you then."

"I don't need you to take me." Freeman started to roll himself backward, out of the room. "I'll be fine on my own."

She followed. "You can't roll yourself up that concrete ramp. It's too steep."

He stopped where he was and looked up at her, clearly amused. "There you go again."

She stopped where she was. "What?"

"You're being bossy. Telling me what I can and can't do. And you've got that tone."

"What tone?"

He eyed her.

She gave a harrumph. "Well, you won't be all that concerned with *my tone* if you try to manage that slope by yourself, roll down that ramp, crash and break your head. Maybe an arm or two. Or maybe the other leg." She pointed. "Then you'll have a matched pair."

"I hadn't thought about how steep the ramp is." He looked up at her, the corner of his mouth turning up in a sheepish smile. "So, maybe I do need a little help."

"I think you do, Freeman," she said, taking on a sickeningly sweet tone. "We wouldn't want you to be injured, now would we?" She came up to his wheelchair and patted him patronizingly on the hand as she might have done an invalid person. She went on with the same singsong voice. "So, I think the *best* thing would be for you to wheel yourself to the foot of the ramp and shout for your hired man to come out and push you up."

She met his gaze and smiled a simpering smile to match the simpering voice.

Freeman took one look at her, burst into laughter and rolled himself out of the parlor. She could still hear him laughing as he went down the hall and she chuckled to herself. She wasn't sure what had just passed between them, but she was certain something had changed. Something for the good, she was quite sure.

Freeman sat on his porch and watched a very short-statured woman climb his steps, carrying a large wicker picnic basket. While he had never met Ellie, he knew this had to be her when he saw her pull into the mill parking lot in a little pony cart. She was the only female little person in the county.

"Hi, I'm Ellie, Katie's friend." She smiled at him. She was so small that they were almost eye-to-eye with him in the wheelchair and her standing. "I live with Sara Yoder and she wanted me to run these canned spiced peaches over. And a fresh-baked blueberry coffee cake."

"Nice to meet you, Ellie." Freeman smiled at her and then called over his shoulder, "Katie, your friend Ellie is here."

"Ellie!" Katie pushed open the kitchen screen door, drying her hands on her apron. She was wearing a scarf, rather than her prayer *kapp,* and wisps of blond hair stuck out here and there, framing her face. He liked her in the scarf; it softened her face. "What a nice surprise."

"I was telling Freeman, this cake just came out of the oven. Sara and I have been baking most of the day," Ellie explained, "and I thought it would be a nice break to get out of the house and drive over here."

"Come sit for a few minutes," Freeman said, indicating the chair to his left.

The little woman, dressed in a bright green dress and starched white *kapp* settled the basket into his lap. "I hope you like blueberries. Because there's blueberry cake and blueberry jam."

"Love them," he assured her. He opened the basket to find the cake, two quarts of peaches and several pints of jam. "This is a real treat," he said. "I know we'll enjoy everything. Tell Sara how much we appreciate her thinking of us."

It was kind of Sara to send the goodies, but secretly, he was a little disappointed. He hadn't been expecting company, and he'd been hoping that he could persuade Katie to take him back over to the mill. He'd finished most of the backed up billing and computer work yesterday when Shad had helped him up the ramp, but he wanted to show her the interior of the mill. It was already Friday afternoon. Somehow the week had gone by in a flash, and there would be two long days before she returned on Monday.

"Did Sara have a good crop of blueberries?" Uncle Jehu asked.

Freeman introduced his uncle. He and Jehu had been sitting there on the porch, enjoying glasses of lemonade and passing the time while Katie cleaned up after the midday meal. Shad had left work early to go to a dentist appointment, and Grossmama was waiting on a customer at the mill. Friday afternoon was usually a busy one, with locals and tourists stopping to buy stone-ground flour, and homemade jams and jellies from the small shop.

"She did," Katie said as she lifted the basket out of his lap. "Sara has a lot of blueberries. We've picked and frozen more blueberries than I've ever seen in my life, and we've eaten our share of them."

"I don't think I've eaten my share," Uncle Jehu said. "And I don't think I ever will."

"Well, I don't want to keep you from your chores, Katie." Ellie turned to her. "I'll just be on my way."

"You don't have to rush off," Freeman insisted, remembering his manners. "Please. Stay a while and sit with us. Katie?" He looked up at her. "Do we have more of that lemonade left?"

"We do," she said. "*Ya*, Ellie. No need to go so soon." She laughed, giving a wave. "Enjoy your summer while you can. Soon enough the *kinder* will be back in school and you'll not have a moment to sit and visit."

Freeman waved the little teacher to one of the chairs at the old table Katie had brought from the shed. He'd thought it far past its prime, but with a good scrubbing and a pretty blue tablecloth, it made the porch look downright inviting. Katie had added mismatched wooden chairs as well and it had become the perfect spot for their evening meals.

Freeman watched Ellie climb up into one of the chairs at the table. She was so short that her feet dangled just like a child's might. She didn't seem to notice. In spite of her size, Ellie was an attractive young woman with a ready smile, bright blue eyes, and blond hair. Katie had spoken of her often, and he knew the two were fast becoming good friends. Any other time, he would have been glad of Ellie's company, but selfishly, with Shad leaving early, he'd been hoping to have some time alone with Katie. He wanted to explain the workings of the mill, and he thought that she'd be interested in its history.

"I'll just cut this cake and we can all have some," Katie offered. "Unless you've had your fill of blueberries," she said to Ellie.

Ellie laughed. "Can't say that I have. Sara has a way with cake."

"I think I'll take a slice over to Ivy," Uncle Jehu said. "And some of that lemonade. No need for her to sit over there alone and miss out on the cake."

"Much traffic on the roads today?" Freeman asked Ellie.

"Not bad," Ellie replied, admiring the fresh cut flowers in a Mason jar in the middle of the table. "These are so pretty. I love black-eyed

Susans." She returned her attention to Freeman. "But I took the back way. And the pony's car-wise."

Katie whisked away the cake and Jehu followed her into the house. Jehu was soon on his way to the mill with cake and lemonade, and Katie brought a tray of refreshments to the table on the porch. Soon the three of them were enjoying the snack. Two more cars pulled into the mill and an English woman got out of the vehicle and took a photograph of Ellie's pony and the cart with her cell phone.

"I wonder if the bishop would object?" Katie asked Freeman.

Ellie laughed, and the two of them began relating a story involving Sara and a tourist at Bylers' Store.

"And then," Ellie explained. "Before the woman knew what had happened, Sara had the woman's camera and was taking a picture of her and her husband. She gave the camera back and hurried away, leaving the Englishers gape-mouthed and without a photo of the quaint little Amish lady."

"At least Sara thought it was funny," Katie said with a giggle. "You don't want to get on her bad side."

"Does she have a temper?" Freeman asked. And at that, both girls laughed even harder. He found himself having a good time, a much better time than he'd expected. He liked watching Katie so at ease and enjoying herself. She looked especially pretty in her tidy scarf and dark green dress. She seemed so happy, and seeing her smile and enjoy herself made him content as well.

Ellie finished her cake and lemonade and the two women carried the empty plates and glasses into the kitchen. Freeman could hear them giggling together like schoolgirls. It was good to hear laughter in the house. For too long, he and his grandmother and uncle had been too serious.

"What's so funny?" he asked when Katie and Ellie came back onto the porch.

Katie looked at her friend and they both giggled again. "Girl stuff," she assured him.

Ellie walked to the steps and then turned to Freeman. "Thank you for the lemonade," she said. "I hope your leg is better soon."

"Thank you." He nodded. "Come again. Any time. You don't even have to bring cake." He flashed a grin. "But you can."

"I'll walk you out to the cart." Katie looped her arm through Ellie's.

Freeman watched them go, talking. Then Ellie climbed up into the cart, picked up the reins and drove out of the yard. Katie stood watching her friend until she pulled onto the road and then returned to the porch.

"What did I miss?" he asked her.

"Wouldn't you like to know?" She giggled. "What do you think of my friend Ellie?"

"I like her," he answered. *But I think I like you better.*

# Chapter Nine

"So you're not going to tell me what was so funny?" Freeman asked Katie as she came up the porch steps.

Katie shook her head. "If we'd wanted you to hear, we would have told you." She cut her eyes at him and teasingly said, "Women's business and not for your ears."

He uttered a disgruntled sigh that she could tell was more for show than genuine disagreement. "Fine hired help you are. Much too saucy." He rested his hands on the rims of his wheelchair. "You should show more respect for the man who pays your wages."

"Should I?" Her blue eyes twinkled. "I suppose you could point out to me a more respectful way of telling you to mind your own beeswax."

He considered that for a moment. "I doubt it."

"So…" She rolled her eyes, enjoying the verbal play between them that she was pretty sure was flirtation. "I suppose I'm being too forward again."

Freeman shook his head. "*Ne*, Katie. In this instance, I'd say you were just right." His smile became a sheepish grin, and she thought again how very attractive he was. Particularly when he smiled. "I had no right to pry about what was said between you and your friend."

"Even when you pay my wages?" she teased. She could feel the telltale heat of a blush washing over her throat and cheeks, but she was having too much fun to back down now. Instead, she fixed him with a penetrating gaze.

And it was Freeman who surrendered. "You have me there." He chuckled. "I'm afraid whatever respect I demanded as your employer is long lost."

"Not lost at all," she assured him, her mood changing to one of all seriousness. "I do respect you, Freeman. Even more for being a man of uncommon good sense."

"Then we're friends?"

She nodded, giving her attention to the folds of her skirt and smoothing it. "Friends." And maybe, she thought, maybe they were just friends. But maybe Ellie was right that it was something more.

Katie definitely wanted it to be more; she was beginning to realize that. But this was unfamiliar ground for her. Unconsciously, she caught a handful of the material in her skirt and gripped it. She'd never had a beau, never understood what her girlfriends meant when they said they were all giddy or had butterflies in their stomach every time they saw the object of their affection. But she certainly didn't feel like herself in Freeman's presence. Was she right that day they'd played horseshoes? Was she falling in love with him?

A mockingbird's trill song sounded loud and clear from the tree by the porch, and the sweetness of it pierced and enhanced her deep musing.

Ellie definitely thought Freeman was interested in her beyond her cooking and housekeeping skills. "Freeman likes you," Ellie had whispered when they'd gone into the kitchen together. "It's as plain as the freckles on your nose."

But if Ellie was right, what did she do about it? Did she do anything? Where did their relationship go from here? And how? What came next? For once in her life, Katie was at a loss.

Freeman gestured toward the entrance to the mill on the far side of the yard, where Ivy and Jehu were standing close together and talking animatedly. "Have you noticed that those two have gotten very friendly lately? More so, I think, since you've come to help out. You've cheered us all up."

She glanced at them and smiled. "More than *friendly*, I think." Her heartbeat slowed to near normal as their conversation turned less personal. "Have you noticed how she watches him when he does his leather work at the kitchen table?" she asked. "And how he perks up whenever she comes into the house? They like each other, all right."

"Of course they do," Freeman said. "Why wouldn't they? We're family. My grandmother is a good woman, and Uncle Jehu, well, he's Uncle Jehu. Who wouldn't like him?"

"I don't mean *like* each other," she explained patiently. "Not as you *like* your friends Charley and Eli, but more than that. The way a man likes a woman and a woman likes a man." She glanced at them. "I think they are both lonely, and it wouldn't take much to convince them that they're good for each other."

"You mean as a couple?" A frown creased his forehead. "But he's younger than she is."

"Not so much that it would be indecent." Katie shrugged. "So your grandmother isn't a young woman. It's no matter. She's still vital and full of life." She considered Freeman for a moment. "Do you have a problem with the idea of the two of them as a couple? Is there some reason you wouldn't want them to court?"

Freeman thought for a minute and then said, "Not really. There are no blood ties between them."

She smiled at him. "So how do we get them together? How do we make them realize how perfect they are for each other?"

Freeman put up his hands, palms out. "We don't. We stay out of their business. It's never wise to interfere."

She brushed away his argument with a wave of her hand. "Nonsense. Ivy probably feels like she can't make the first move, even if she wants to. And your uncle is shy. We have to find a way to get them together, to help them see that marriage would be in the best interest of them both."

*"Marriage?"* He looked at her as if she'd just said the most absurd thing. "You want me to try and convince my grandmother and my uncle to marry each other?"

She chuckled at his typically male reluctance to grasp what she'd been trying to tell him. "Who else are we talking about? Of course, to each other."

He shook his head slowly, though she could

tell he was thinking about the idea. "It sounds like trouble to me," he said.

She folded her arms. "But you agree with me that they're perfect for each other."

"I didn't say that."

"Freeman." She sighed and let her arms fall to her sides. "You know I'm right. Admit it. How many men do you know who would think to carry cake and lemonade to a woman? And doesn't Ivy always laugh at Uncle Jehu's jokes, no matter how many times she's heard them?"

"That's a good point," he agreed. "She does laugh at his jokes." He looked up at her. "So you think that the two of us should endeavor to bring them together?"

"I do," she said. "They deserve to be happy."

Freeman looked doubtful. "And you know what would make them happy?"

"It's a natural thing; God meant us to walk on this earth two by two. She's widowed and he's alone, too. They need someone and they like each other. Why shouldn't they marry?"

He sat there for a moment and then looked up at her. "I guess we've come to the conclusion that there's no reason why they shouldn't. What I'm unconvinced of is that we should have a hand in trying to unite them. I've always believed in minding my own affairs and letting others mind theirs."

"Even when it would bring about something good and positive?"

"Your opinion," he reminded her.

She frowned. "If you're so set against them finding happiness together, then you should certainly stay out of it." She was quiet for a moment and then went on. "I know they aren't my relatives, although I've come to care for them both in the past several weeks. But…" She drew in a deep breath and forged ahead. "I won't be here after today, so I suppose you're right. It's foolish of me to talk about us trying to support a courtship between them."

"What do you mean you won't be here?" He scowled. Then it dawned on him what she meant. "Wait. You've been here two weeks already? I don't think that's right."

"*Ya*, it's been two weeks," she told him.

"Well, I…" He stopped and started again. "I may have agreed to two weeks, but that was only supposed to be a trial. Sara must have told you the job would likely be longer than just the two weeks. You can't leave us now, Katie. I'm not ready to run this household yet. I'm not back on my feet yet. Who would do the washing? And cooking? I don't think Grossmama's oatmeal would be good for my recovery."

She averted her gaze, pressing her lips together in amusement. Obviously, Freeman didn't want her to leave. She wondered if she should tell him that talk of oatmeal might not be the best way to convince her. But the truth was, she didn't want to leave either. "I suppose I could stay on another week," she offered, looking back to him. "If you're certain you can't manage without me."

"Another two weeks, at least, and not a day less."

"I don't know—" she hemmed, mostly because she didn't know that she should give in too quickly to his demands. He was just becoming bearable to live with. She didn't want to put any ideas in his head that he could tell her what to do.

"No buts, Katie," Freeman insisted, though not unkindly. "If it's a matter of how much we're paying you, then we can renegotiate."

She shook her head, aghast that he should think that she was greedy. "It was never the money, Freeman. What you pay is more than fair."

He nodded. "Good. Then there will be no more talk of you leaving us yet. I'll expect you back promptly on Monday morning."

Katie tried to hide her delight. He wanted her to stay as much as she wanted to be there. "*Ya,* Freeman, if you think that's best," she murmured before looking up at him through her lashes. "But there's one stipulation. If I do come back for another two weeks, you'll let me move that bed out of the kitchen. It...it's too..." She grimaced. "It takes up too much room and it gathers dust. You'll get far better rest in one of the downstairs bedrooms."

"Agreed." He nodded. "So you'll stay on at least another two weeks. It's settled."

She lowered her gaze to her bare feet. If he saw her eyes, he'd know how pleased she was. She wanted to shout with joy—rush down to the millpond and leap in, fully dressed. She was staying on here with Freeman, Jehu and Ivy.

"And maybe there's one more condition," she ventured.

"Oh? Another?" His voice showed amusement. "What more could you ask of me?"

"That you'll consider what I said about your grandmother and your uncle. That you'll think about helping me find ways to make them see how much they need each other."

He stroked his chin. He was clean-shaven, but he'd missed a spot on the left and a small clump of reddish whiskers had sprung up. She found the mishap as endearing as his argument for keeping her on in order to avoid his grandmother's oatmeal.

"I'll think about it," Freeman allowed. "But I'm making no promises."

"That's all I ask," she said. "Because, if you do think about it, I know you'll come to the conclusion that I'm right."

"Woman, have you ever considered that you usually think you're in the right?"

She smiled sweetly. "It's because I am. And you know it."

The following morning dawned rainy and wet, but it didn't stop Freeman from repeatedly wheeling himself to the screen door to look out into the yard. Uncle Jehu was at the sink washing the breakfast dishes, and Ivy had gone to the mill to tend the store.

"Your coffee's getting cold, boy," his uncle warned. "What are you doing by the door? Katie doesn't come again until Monday."

"I'm not looking for Katie," Freeman answered, trying to ignore the fact that his uncle called him a boy. He knew it was said out of affection, but it still rubbed like a rough spot under a harness. Maybe Katie was right. Maybe it would be better for them all if Uncle Jehu married his grandmother and he moved into her house and out of this one. Maybe they were too much in each other's shoes for comfort.

"So who are you expecting?" Uncle Jehu persisted.

Freeman tried to find patience. His uncle's

curiosity was normal enough. But it made it hard when a man could find no privacy with a delicate matter in his own house. Did he always have to discuss everything with his uncle and his grandmother?

"Too wet for horseshoes," Jehu said when Freeman didn't answer right away. "Not Eli or Charley. The way that wind smells, it will rain all day and into the night." He found a clean hand towel to dry the bowls and spoons on the sideboard.

"You're right. No horseshoes today," Freeman agreed.

Uncle Jehu dropped the clean spoons into the knife and fork drawer. "Make for damp traveling to church tomorrow. Not too far. At Big Peachy's. Not too far to walk for Ivy and me, but if it's still wet, we'll take the buggy." He turned his head as he would if he were sighted. "Unless you've a mind to come to worship with us. Then we'd take the buggy regardless of the weather."

Freeman shook his head. "I'd not thought to go. It would be too much to ask for someone to come for me on the Sabbath. Help me in and out of a buggy. Too much," he repeated.

"It must be a trial to you, missing service and the company of the community." Uncle Jehu carefully hung the towel on a hook near the sink. "Not to mention Big Peachy's wife's raisin-nut bread." He grinned. "I'll smuggle you home a few slices if there are any left after the second sitting."

Freeman nodded. He'd missed several Sabbaths since the accident and it did trouble him. All his life church Sundays had been a solid part of his life, and he found it difficult to stay at home while his grandmother and uncle went to worship and to hear the word of God as revealed to the preachers and the bishop.

"So who are you expecting this morning?" Uncle Jehu persisted. "Some of the church elders come to bring you spiritual comfort?"

Freeman gritted his teeth. He should have just told his uncle, but he hadn't been sure he was ready to speak his intentions aloud. Not that he could go on much longer that way. If he didn't speak his intentions, how would he ever know what chance he had? "Sara Yoder," he answered under his breath.

"What's that?" Jehu touched his ear.

Freeman knew very well his uncle had heard him. "I'm expecting Sara Yoder."

"The matchmaker?"

"Yes," Freeman agreed reluctantly. "The matchmaker. I sent word by way of Shad last night. I'm expecting her this morning."

"And you had Shad take this message? Not

Katie, even with her staying at Sara's house?" Freeman's uncle's mouth twitched into a smile. "Why would that be?"

Freeman sighed with resignation. He should have known there would be no way to do this privately. Not with him still laid up. "Because I didn't want Katie to know anything about it. I have business with Sara."

*"Ach."* The older man nodded as he settled into a chair at the table, where he'd already arranged some of his leather working tools and a partially finished pony bridle. "Well, it's about time."

Freeman didn't respond.

Jehu picked up a leather punch and rolled the head between his fingers, feeling for the correct prong. "You know, you couldn't do better than Katie. You should have taken a wife years ago."

"I didn't say I wanted to speak to Sara about Katie."

This time it was Jehu who didn't respond.

"Okay...I want to talk to her about Katie," Freeman conceded.

Jehu searched for the right piece of leather. "Couldn't you just ask the girl to walk out with you yourself?"

"It's not that simple, Uncle. Picking a woman to live with for the rest of your life is serious business. I don't want to make a mistake I'll live to regret."

His uncle scoffed. "You're talking about *her*, now. Not Katie. The one who left you at the altar."

"She didn't leave me at the altar," Freeman answered testily. *But it was close enough.* "I made a mistake once. How do I know that I'm not doing the same thing again? I want to talk to the matchmaker because…she knows about these things."

His uncle frowned. "That was ten years ago. Susan's happily married with three children. It's time you let her go."

"I'm trying. It's not so easy." He considered how much more to say, and then went on. "I'm afraid I don't know my own mind. How do I know that I'm not grasping at straws, trying to convince myself that I could be happy with Katie because I'm lonely and need a wife and she's a good cook?"

"*Are* you just interested in Katie just for her cooking skills?"

"Of course not," Freeman said. "She's kind and clever and she understands me. She understands my ways. And she makes me laugh. I like that she makes me laugh," he said as much to himself as to his uncle. "And there's something about her that…" He didn't finish the sentence, because he didn't know how to explain the way she made him feel. It was as if when she was there with him, everything seemed right in the world and when she wasn't there, it was if something was missing, not from the mill, but his heart.

"Sounds like you've about made up your mind about Katie." Jehu nodded. "Or you wouldn't have wanted to meet with Sara about her."

"You know how I am," he explained. "I need all the facts. I don't want to make a fool of myself. Sara's introduced Katie to prospective suitors, and there's some sort of arrangement with a farmer in Kentucky. I just want to know what's what. Not that I've made up my mind or anything."

"There's no betrothal or they would have said so. I know Sara. She wouldn't have sent the girl if she'd been spoken for."

Freeman wheeled his chair around to face his uncle. "Are you saying Sara Yoder set this up? Set *me* up? That that's why she sent Katie here to begin with?"

"Who's to say what goes on in a woman's mind? I asked Sara to make a recommendation for a housekeeper and I might have mentioned that I was concerned about the fact that you were still single. But I don't know why she sent Katie." His uncle laid down the bridle with a shrug. "What I do know is that you better snatch Katie up fast before it's too late." He chuckled. "Then you'll not have to eat your grandmother's oatmeal for breakfast every day for the rest of your life." He got to his feet. "I think I'll take myself along to the mill. See if Ivy's in a better mood than you are."

"Good idea," Freeman said. "She enjoys your company."

"Does she?" Uncle Jehu asked, turning to his nephew. "She tell you that?"

"*Ne*. But I know her."

Jehu seemed to think on that as he placed his tools and the bridle back in a small leather chest. "Sounds like a horse and buggy just turned into the yard," he remarked. "That will be your matchmaker."

"And…"

"And?" Jehu asked, standing there.

"You said you were just leaving," Freeman reminded him.

"So I was. Good luck with Sara." Chuckling to himself, Jehu left the house.

Sara soon came up the porch steps in her cloak and black church bonnet, both splotched with dark spots of water. "Fit weather out there for ducks," she said, walking into the house as Freeman held the screen door open for her.

"I appreciate you coming over, Sara. I'm still not quite up to traveling." Freeman fought his nervousness as she hung her bonnet and cape over the back of a chair before he ushered her to the table. "Would you like coffee?" he asked.

For ten minutes they exchanged neighborly talk about crops and coming school fund-raisers and a visiting bishop from the Midwest who'd preached recently in Seven Poplars. And then, when all the polite greetings and inquiries after the families' health and the likelihood of abundant crops had been given and received, and he was feeling a little calmer, he turned to the important matter of Katie's availability.

Better now than never, Freeman thought. "I imagine you know why I asked you here."

"I can guess. Katie," she said simply.

"Katie," he repeated, his nervousness coming back to him in one great flood. "Sara, I don't know how this works," he admitted. "I've not brought up my—" he cleared his throat "—interest in Katie to her. She told me that there's a man in Kentucky who wants to marry her. But she said nothing about a firm commitment."

Sara tented her hands on the table. "Katie's a fine young woman. She'd make you a proper wife."

"So you think we're well-suited to each other?" he asked, unable to hide his excitement.

Sara looked at him with those dark eyes of hers. "I just said that, didn't I?"

"I've not made up my mind, of course," he hedged. "I wouldn't want to have you think otherwise. I'm just trying to find out the lay of the land, as it were. Do you know how she feels about me? I wouldn't want to approach her if there was no chance she…" He felt heat rise on the back of his neck. "If she wouldn't be interested in me."

Sara smiled. "So there *is* an attraction on your part? I can't say I'm surprised." She looked around the kitchen. "She seems to have done a fine job in here. I saw Jehu on the way in and he speaks highly of her."

Freeman's eyes narrowed. He had suspected Sara might have had an ulterior motive when she chose Katie to be his housemaid. Now he was afraid they'd all been in on it: Sara, Jehu… maybe even his grandmother. But that wasn't a good reason to change his mind; he had enough sense to know that. "She said something about you communicating with the man in Kentucky. I'm not hiring you as a matchmaker," he said. "If I do decide to pay court to her, it wouldn't be fair or right for you to expect a fee from me as well."

Sara laughed. "I can't say for sure if Katie would accept an offer from you to court her, but I *can* tell you that your pocketbook is safe. Whatever arrangement I may or may not have made with Katie's family, or a man's family in Kentucky, you and I have no such arrangement."

He pushed his wheelchair a little from the table, his nervousness rising again. "Are you saying there's a betrothal agreement with this man in Kentucky?"

"There is a firm offer for a betrothal, in writing," Sara replied. "Katie is in the process of deciding whether or not she will go visit him and his family and see what's what."

He dared a glance at Sara's pretty, round face. "So what you're saying is that if I wanted to ask her to consider walking out with me, it's not too late?"

"That's something that you'll have to ask her. You know our Katie." Sara shrugged, but her dark eyes sparkled with amusement. "She's a woman who knows her own mind."

# Chapter Ten

"I've always liked the way the mill smells," Freeman said to Katie as he took in the cavernous interior of the mill with a sweeping gesture. "Molasses, grain and water."

"Me, too," she agreed. She pushed his wheelchair closer to the now motionless grindstones. She'd worn a new lavender-colored dress today, with a white apron over it, and the simple lines of the plain but neatly-sewn garments gave her a wholesome look that was accented by her crisp white *kapp*. He couldn't keep from looking up at her. He'd missed her all weekend. Missed her more than he was comfortable with.

Their voices echoed slightly, taking him back ten years to another beautiful woman who'd stood beside him in this room, bringing bittersweet memories of someone he'd rather forget. Susan had been equally pretty, but in a much more delicate way, dark where Katie was fair, soft-spoken and modest rather than brash. And the contrast didn't end there. Being alone with him in the vast mill, with massive oak beams, shadowy corners and fluttering pigeons in the rafters had unnerved Susan. She'd been uncomfortable here, even a little frightened, but Katie gave no such impression. Instead, she appeared to be enjoying the experience as much as he was. Encouraged by her eagerness, Freeman pushed thoughts of Susan to the furthest recesses of his mind.

The huge millstones were motionless, the mechanism silent, but in his mind Freeman could almost hear the familiar churn of the waterwheel, the whoosh of tumbling grain down the chute, and the grinding rumble of the granite stones. Along the walls, baskets of corn waited to be ground into meal. A fine dusting of wheat flour coated the wide pine floorboards and every visible surface. There was too much dust to suit Freeman and he frowned. "Shad should have swept this up this morning. Wheat dust is highly explosive under the right conditions. The boy may not have the brains to make a miller."

"No one's complained about the quality of your flour while you've been laid up," Katie observed. "Shad's young yet, and as you say, there's a lot to learn. Maybe you're too hard on him."

He opened his mouth to reply, then closed it, mostly because he didn't want to argue with her, and maybe because he knew she was at least half-right.

Katie wandered over to run a palm over the furrowed surface of a millstone that rested against one wall and stared up nearly three stories at the hand-hewn oak rafters barely visible in the semi-darkness. This section of the structure soared from where they stood to the hand-cut cedar shingled roof. Two-thirds of the first floor supported a second story containing the granary.

He pointed to a metal chute that ran from the grain bins to the wooden hopper above the millstones. "If I pull this lever, grain comes down the hopper into this mechanism called the shoe."

Katie returned to stand beside his wheelchair as he pointed out the control that would open the gate on the sluice box, sending a flow of water over the wheel and bringing the mill to life. Freeman knew that he was running on, perhaps boring her with the details of turning corn, wheat and rye to flour and animal feed. He kept sneaking glances at her, half expecting to see her eyes glaze over as he prattled on about the proper distances you had to keep the rotating millstone above the fixed one for different processes. But, to his surprise, Katie listened intently to what he was saying.

"Shad has been grinding horse feed this morning, a special order for a customer who keeps a stable of harness horses west of Dover."

Katie nodded. "I've seen his truck hauling away the bags of feed."

"*Ya*, English. A good customer."

He was surely prattling now. What was wrong with him? His uncle's advice to seriously consider Katie only added to his own conclusion that she was the right woman. And his talk with Sara Yoder had gone well. Now was the time to speak up, to ask Katie if he was someone she would consider courting. Courting wouldn't commit him to marrying her. Either of them could change their mind. So where was his nerve? Why was he going on about milling rather than speaking up about what was really on his mind?

The night before, he'd hardly slept for mulling the question over and over in his head. Was he making the right decision? Should he ask her to walk out with him? Maybe it would be a mistake. If he asked to court her and she turned him down flat, it would be impossible for her to go on working here. It would be too uncomfortable for them both. That would mean that she would go away, and he might not see her again.

But if he asked and she agreed, how could he be sure that he wasn't making another huge mistake like he had with Susan? Englisher couples might divorce after marriage if they were unhappy, but the Amish did not. They would be bound to each other for better or worse for the rest of their lives. There were issues with Katie's forceful personality that worried him. He didn't want to repeat his parents' mistakes in their marriage. His mother had ruled the house, making all the decisions while his father did whatever she told him. Was that what he wanted?

The loud flapping of wings and a hoarse caw broke through his thoughts and he turned to see what was causing the disturbance. Katie's reaction was even quicker than his. She hurried to a corner of the room near a dirty window. "Shoo, kitty," she cried, clapping her hands.

A tiger-striped barn cat streaked away, ears flattened and crooked tail giving away the animal's identity. It was Mustard, a half-grown stray that Freeman had rescued from a watery grave when some heartless person had thrown him out of a car window into the millpond. The weighted bag had landed in shallow water, and Freeman, fishing along the wooded bank, had heard the pitiful cries of the drowning cat and adopted him.

But Katie had no eyes for the cat. Her attention was fixed on a black, feathered object crouching against the dusky wall. "It's a crow," she pronounced. "I think he's injured. Poor thing."

Black eyes gleamed as the bird hopped back, nearly losing its balance. "Don't get too close," Freeman cautioned. "The state officials say that there's bird flu around. Crows are one of the types of birds that are most often affected."

*"Ne."* She crouched down to get a better look at the crow. "He isn't sick. I think he has a broken leg. See how he doesn't put any weight on it? And the good leg is tangled in a length of corn string."

One of the bird's wings drooped and his feathers were ruffled. "He must have had a fight with the cat and come out second-best." Freeman wondered why the crow had come into the mill. Pigeons made their home here and they came and went through openings in the eaves. And sometimes owls nested in the granary, attracted by the mice that the cats missed, but he'd never seen a crow in here.

"Look how it's watching us," Katie said. "He's frightened, but brave."

He rolled his chair a little closer to see. "I

think the string is knotted around his foot. Poor thing. Crows are said to be among the most intelligent of birds." He looked at Katie. "It could be that I could put a splint on his hurt leg. But don't think I can catch it. It may fly if I come any closer."

Katie stood up and looked at him. "You would try to heal it? A crow?"

He nodded, only slightly embarrassed at his show of tenderness. "I've always had an unnatural softness for creatures," he admitted. "Abandoned cats, mostly, but a few dogs, the donkey past his prime that you see grazing in the pasture, a blind ox. Once I even brought home a skunk that had been hit by a car. But my *mam* put a stop to that. Out went the skunk, and me with it. She made me bathe in tomato juice and shaved my hair as bald as an onion. Still I stank for months." He shrugged. "The bishops say animals have no souls, but they feel hunger and pain as we do. Surely a merciful God would expect us to do what we can to lesson their suffering if we can."

"I agree," she said untying her apron.

"Don't—" he began, but before he could finish, she'd thrown the apron over the crow and gathered the struggling bird up in it.

"Shh, shh," she soothed, cradling the bundle against her.

The crow gave a hissing croak and quieted. "Let me see that leg," Freeman said. She came closer so that he could examine the crow's legs. One leg was bent unnaturally and when he felt it, it seemed as though he could feel the bone move as if it was broken. The good leg had a corn string knotted tightly around it, cutting into the flesh. Freeman removed his penknife from his pocket and carefully sliced away the strands. The skin was broken but the injury to this leg didn't seem severe. "That's better," he said. "It had to be painful."

Katie crooned to the bird as she might a sick child. "Be still," she murmured. "It will be better. I promise."

"Don't make promises you can't keep," Freeman warned. He was touched by the kindness in her eyes and the fearless way she held the crow. "And be careful. He has a sharp beak."

"What makes you think it's a male?" she asked. "I don't think you can tell just by looking at him."

"Male or female, it makes no matter. And I have to call him something. Let's take *him* to the house and see what we can do for the break."

"If you think that's best, Freeman," she murmured, smiling up at him with shining eyes. She passed the bird to him, and he held it gently, so close he could feel the frightened beating of the creature's heart. But the crow had stopped fighting against the encompassing apron.

"It's afraid," he said. "Fetch one of those empty baskets, the one with the lid." She did as he instructed and they placed the bird in it and fastened the lid.

"You hold the basket," Katie said as she took hold of the wheelchair handles to push him back to the house. "You don't want to drop him and break the other leg."

Freeman glanced back over his shoulder at her and felt something shift within his chest. He exhaled slowly, certain of his mind now, certain that he was already half in love with this kind young woman. He'd made a bad choice when he'd courted Susan, but Katie was nothing like Susan. He couldn't imagine Susan getting anywhere near an injured crow. So maybe he and Susan had been too different. Maybe losing her to another man was God's way of leading him to a happy marriage. To Katie.

"Wait," he said when they reached the bottom of the ramp. "Stop pushing."

"What's wrong?" Katie slowed the chair to a halt.

"I have something I need to talk to you about." He felt short of breath. "Don't laugh," he said.

She walked around his chair to face him. "I won't," she promised. She waited.

Freeman wasn't sure what to say. He only knew that he had to say something and this was the time to say it.

"What is it, Freeman?" she asked when still he hesitated. She waited and then said, "You know you can talk to me about anything. Friends talk to each other."

"That…that's just it, Katie. I was hoping… I wanted to ask…" He looked down at his cast and then up at her again. "I was hoping you see me as more than just a friend."

The crow scratched at the bottom of the basket and croaked feebly. Katie took the basket from him and placed it on the ground. When she stood upright again, she looked him squarely in the eyes. "What are you trying to say?"

"Well…we get along, don't we?" His heart raced. If only he wasn't stuck in this chair. Surely, he'd have more courage to speak his mind if he could stand on his own two feet.

She nodded, her expression showing that she was clearly puzzled.

"So I was wondering if you…I mean…if we could see if…"

Katie waited, surprising him with her patience while he attempted to untangle his tongue.

"I was wondering if you would consider letting me court you," he said in a rush, his voice louder and more forceful than he'd intended.

Her eyes widened. "Are you serious?" Then she clapped both hands over her mouth. "You mean it?" she asked, her words muffled.

He couldn't tell if she was for or against, for sure. "J-just to see," he stammered. "A trial walking out. So we'd know if we're…" He exhaled heavily. Susan was the only other woman he had ever walked out with. When he had asked her, it had come so easily. He didn't know why he was finding this so hard.

She lowered her hands. "So we're not talking about officially courting but a…*trial* courting?" She was grinning ear to ear. "To see if we actually *want* to court?" she asked.

He nodded. "Exactly," he said, relieved she understood what he was making such a mess of saying.

"Freeman!" she cried and flung herself at him, neatly missing his cast and wrapping her arms around his neck and kissing him full on the mouth. "*Ya*! Of course I would. I could. I didn't think you—" She broke off and kissed him again, this time a tender and sweet caress. "Oh, Freeman," she whispered. "I'd love for you to court me."

"Katie." She smelled as sweet and fresh as she looked. He loved the feel of her pressed against him and the taste of her lips. "Katie," he repeated, unable to say anything else.

This time, it was she who became shy, suddenly pulling back. "That was inappropriate, wasn't it?"

He clamped the brake on the wheelchair and pushed himself up, awkwardly standing on one foot. "Maybe," he allowed breathily. "But I liked it just fine."

"So…" She backed away from him, her face radiant. "We've agreed? A *trial* courtship? You and me?"

He nodded. "Agreed." He reached out a hand to her, hoping that she would kiss him again. Instead, she snatched up the basket with the crow and fled the mill.

"Katie," he called after her. And then he was laughing too and savoring the sound of her name on his lips.

"He seems very nice, your miller," Patsy remarked as she formed ground beef into patties. She was chubby and tow-haired, with thick glasses, a pointed chin, and a kind disposition. Katie thought she was the perfect wife for her brother Isaac. "A pity about his broken leg," Patsy continued. "But by the grace of God he wasn't killed by that bull."

Patsy, Katie and a group of friends were

gathered in the kitchen of Katie's childhood home, preparing for a barbecue. Some of those who'd come were married women, some walking out with prospective husbands, and others, like Ellie, hoping to find someone special. It had been Katie's brother Isaac's idea to host a birthday celebration for his wife Patsy. They'd invited two dozen guests, including Katie and Freeman, Ellie, Nona, who was one of Patsy's sisters, and Thomas Stutzman.

Since all of the guests were in their twenties and thirties, Katie's mother had gone visiting for the day to allow the young people to enjoy themselves without an older member of the community dampening their fun. Isaac had promised volleyball, men against the women, as well as an archery contest, and fast hymn singing. They would stuff themselves with picnic food, splash in the farm pond and drink homemade ginger ale until dark, when Isaac had promised that they would have a bonfire, complete with hot dogs and marshmallows to roast.

"If Freeman has a fault, it's that he has his own way of doing things," Katie observed as she cut a pan of still-warm brownies into squares. "He's so nice, though. I still can't believe we're walking out together. It's so new that it doesn't seem real. At first, when I went there to help with the housework, I thought Freeman was difficult, but after you get to know him, he's really sweet."

Ellie paused from slicing a watermelon into wedges, smiling mischievously. "Now she says *difficult*. I won't tell you what she called him that first day when she got home. But I knew she must like him. All she could talk about was Freeman this and Freeman that."

Katie chuckled. "*Ya*, I did say he was grumpy."

Patsy's older sister Meta, married three years and about to give birth to her second child, was as plump and cheerful as the birthday girl. "The same with her." She pointed a mayonnaise-covered spoon in Patsy's direction and motioned with it to emphasize her words. "Our *mam* said that if Isaac didn't ask to marry her soon, she would drive over herself and fix it up with his mother because Patsy was so *narrish* over him that she couldn't toast bread without burning it."

"I never called Isaac grumpy," Patsy protested. "He doesn't have a grumpy bone in his body." She looked at Katie for support. "Does he?"

Katie shook her head. "*Ne*. As brothers go, I've been blessed."

Almost as if he'd known they were talking about him, Isaac appeared outside the kitchen window. "That food almost ready?" he asked. "I'd like to get the hamburgers on the grill. I'm starved."

"You're always starved," Katie teased.

"*Ya*. Fortunately, my new wife is a *goot* cook." Patsy blushed with pleasure as he winked at her. "I'm waiting for those baked beans of yours," he said.

"We'll be ready in two shakes of a lamb's tail," Katie told him. "Hold off for a few more minutes, and there will be enough to fill even you."

"But maybe not Thomas," he teased.

"*Ya,*" Patsy said. "Even Thomas." And the women all laughed.

Katie had been delighted when Freeman had eventually agreed to accept Isaac's invitation. He'd been stuck at home for weeks, and he needed an outing. With Shad and Uncle Jehu's help, she'd gotten Freeman into the buggy at the mill. He'd been able to drive the horse, something that pleased him immensely. And when they'd arrived at her home, Isaac and Thomas had been all too willing to assist him in getting out and into his wheelchair. The doctor had promised that Freeman would soon be on crutches, and he was eagerly looking forward to it. Freeman was outside with the men now; she could hear snatches of his laughter through the open windows.

"He has a fine business," Meta said. "Your Freeman? The mill?"

Katie nodded. She supposed he was considered a good catch, but she hadn't thought at all about what he had. It was who he was that was important. That, and the way she felt when they were together. All the way here, they'd laughed and talked, with Freeman showing her a fun side of his personality that she was just coming to appreciate.

"So, I suppose you're calling it off with that man in Kentucky," Jane asked. She and Thomas, Ellie's friend, had the same last name but weren't related.

"Of course," Katie replied. "It wouldn't be fair to Uriah not to tell him that I was going with someone."

Jane giggled. "Two men wanting to court you at the same time—that must be something."

"I wish Victor hadn't brought that stranger," Ellie commented, glancing out the window as she handed a plate of watermelon wedges to Jane.

"Who?" Katie asked, looking out the window, too. "His cousin Jakob? The blacksmith from Indiana?"

"Yes, Jakob. Just because he's little like me, everyone will think we're meant for each other."

"What's wrong with him?" Jane asked. "He seems pleasant enough, and Victor says he's the best farrier he's ever seen. Just because he isn't as tall as—"

"Ellie," Meta admonished, "I've never heard you talk bad about anyone. How can you find fault with him for being…small when—"

"When I am?" Ellie sighed with exasperation. "You have no idea what it's like. How my parents searched far and wide for a short husband for me. One was an Old Order Mennonite boot maker from Ontario."

"Something wrong with boot makers?" Patsy asked. "At least you'd always have good shoes with soles on them."

Ellie rolled her eyes. "He was in his fifties and had eleven children. A good man, I'm sure, but not for me. I'm not marrying someone just because he's little like me." She rested her small hands on her hips. "I was born Amish and I stay Amish. I don't care if God's love leads others to a different path, but that's not for me. I could never wed a man, dwarf or giant, who didn't share my own path."

"No one's asking you to marry Jakob," Jane said. "Just to welcome him to our community. We can use another blacksmith and far-rier now that Thomas has made it plain it's not for him."

"You needn't worry about that," Katie said, coming to her friend's defense. "I've never known Ellie to be unkind to anyone, and cer-tainly not unwelcoming to a newcomer."

*"Ne,"* Ellie said, shaking her head. "I de-served that. I said what I shouldn't. Naturally, I won't be rude to Jakob. Just don't expect me to ride home with him."

Meta laughed. "We won't, not when Thomas is around. The way he looks at you, I'm think-ing he'll be popping the question soon."

Ellie shook her head. "I don't know why ev-eryone keeps saying that. Thomas and I are just friends."

"Well, *friends*, if we don't get out there with this food, the men will all be at the door want-ing to know where it is," Katie reminded them.

The afternoon and evening were as much fun as she'd hoped. Because he was confined to the wheelchair, Freeman couldn't participate in the games, but Isaac and the others made certain he wasn't left out. They asked him to officiate at the volleyball match and archery contests. Later, when everyone gathered around the fire to make s'mores, Katie sat beside him and let him hold her hand in the semi-darkness.

"I'm glad we came," he said.

"Me, too," Katie agreed. Today had been one of the best days of her life. Her skirt was still damp from where she'd waded in the pond, and she'd come in third behind Thomas and Isaac at archery. Best of all, Freeman had cheered loudly for her. Now, here in the semi-darkness with the navy-blue sky arching overhead, the bright scattering of stars, and the warmth of Freeman's touch, she was almost giddy with happiness.

"I wish we were riding home together," he whispered to her. "I wish I could take you back to Sara's myself."

She didn't answer. She wished it, too, but it was late, and she knew that he was tired and probably in pain from being up all day. Thomas had invited her to ride back to Sara's with the two of them, and Ellie had insisted.

"I like your brother and sister-in-law," Freeman said, still holding her hand tightly.

She smiled, glad that they had hit it off. "You did so well traveling today that you'll be ready for church next week," she said. "It's time."

*"Ya,"* he agreed. "It is time, but there's only one way I could possibly go."

"Oh?" She met his warm gaze.

*"Ya."* He grinned, bringing his nose very close to hers. "You have to come with me."

# Chapter Eleven

Katie met his gaze in the darkness, the firelight flickering light and dark against his features. "You want me to come to church with you?" she asked, her throat tight with emotion. "Then, everyone would know that we..."

"That we're together?" His warm chuckle was a comforting hug that brought tears to her eyes. "That we're courting? We are, aren't we? I thought that was settled." He squeezed her hand again and then released it.

She struggled to find words to convey her desire to go with him, but not to rush what might be an enormous commitment. "I *would* like to come to worship with you, but this is so new. I thought..." She didn't finish her sentence. What did she think? She thought they'd agreed they would merely consider a formal courtship. But she also thought that she'd never been happier in her life than she was right now. With Freeman.

"Not having second thoughts, are you?" he asked. His tone was teasing, but he genuinely wanted to know what she was thinking.

She shook her head, shifting in the lawn chair. "*Ne*, Freeman. This feels right. I've been praying, and…I think this is what was supposed to happen. I've been so happy since I've come to work for you at the mill house, and I love your family. And…" She almost said "And I love you," but kept the words to herself, not quite ready to speak them.

"Good, because we're a package. If you marry me, you accept Grossmama and Uncle Jehu. And he will continue living with us as long as he wants."

She placed a marshmallow on a green willow switch and held it over the coals of the fire. Everyone else was gathered around the fire, too, talking and laughing, but she felt like it was just the two of them. "I understand, and I'm fine with it. I always imagined myself living with extended family. I think it's the way we should all live. But you know, he and Ivy could come to their own arrangement. If they decide to marry, I'm sure Ivy will want Jehu to move into her house."

He looked amused. "They aren't even court-ing. How can you have them married already?"

She laughed. "Of course they're courting. Men." She shook her head again. "You see ev-erything and understand nothing about a wom-an's heart." Her marshmallow flamed up and she withdrew the stick and blew on it. "Oh," she exclaimed. "It's burned."

"Just the way I like it," Freeman steered the stick toward him and leaned over to take a bite.

"Careful," she cautioned. "It's hot. You'll—"

"Ah!" he said, touching his lip. "It's hot." A dribble of marshmallow fell onto his chin.

"I warned you," she teased. "But you never listen to reason."

He dabbed at the melted marshmallow and rubbed his sticky finger on the tip of her nose. "Now everyone will wonder what we've been up to."

He laughed, and she laughed with him.

"How will I get this off?" she asked, rubbing at the sticky, warm marshmallow on her face.

"Fortunately for you, I come prepared." He removed a clean handkerchief from his trouser pocket and gave it to her.

She moistened the corner of his handker-chief with a little of the water in her glass and wiped away the marshmallow on her nose.

"Now you," she said. Obediently, he allowed her to clean his chin.

"Satisfied?" he asked, leaning closer to her than he probably should have.

"Hey, Ellie," Thomas called loudly from beside them. "I dare you to go into the pond again."

"What? Wading in the dark?" Ellie's laughter rang out.

"If you go, I'll go," Thomas dared.

Amid a flurry of giggles and excited calls, Thomas and Ellie and then the rest of the party left the bonfire and moved toward the pond, leaving Katie and Freeman alone.

"You can go if you want," Freeman offered.

"*Ne*, I like it fine where I am," Katie said. She placed another marshmallow on the end of her willow bough. "I'll try not to burn this one," she promised.

"Actually, I'm glad they left us alone," he said. "There's something I've been wanting to tell you."

"Something bad or good?"

"Nothing that changes anything between us. At least, I hope not," he replied. "It's just… something I need to tell you. Something you need to know and I wanted you to know from me, before you hear it from anyone else."

A ripple of apprehension slid down her spine,

and she pulled the marshmallow back out of the heat before it had even started to blister. "Okay."

"Ten years ago, I thought I was in love with someone," he said quietly. "We were planning to marry."

Katie sat quietly for a moment. Freeman was older than she was; she wasn't silly enough to think he had never taken a girl home from a singing or escorted someone to a picnic or a fund-raiser, but it wasn't as easy to hear from him as she had thought it would be. "What was her name?" she asked quietly.

"Susan."

"And you and Susan courted?"

"We did, for the better part of a year. Then she broke it off and chose someone else." He shrugged. "End of story."

"And you've never courted anyone since?"

"I took a few girls home from singings, but nothing serious. No."

"So that's why you've remained single so long." Katie's mouth felt dry and she picked up her glass to take a sip of water. "You must have cared for her very much."

"I did. She married him, moved to Ohio, and they have three children. As far as I know, they've been happy together."

"But she hurt you," Katie said softly.

He took his time responding. "She did. And maybe I used my hurt to avoid moving on, starting the family that everyone expected, but whatever it is, it doesn't matter anymore. But I wouldn't have felt right not telling you."

She nodded. "I'm so glad you did." *Ten years.* Sad, she thought, that Freeman had mourned his lost love so long. She hesitated, trying to push down the curiosity that a woman would naturally feel for an old rival. She reached for another marshmallow from the bag in the grass. "Is it okay if I ask you…what she was like?"

"Of course." He chuckled. "She was nothing like you, Katie, if that's what you're asking. Nothing at all. Petite, soft-spoken, gentle and biddable. As far from you as December is from July."

She thrust her marshmallow back into the fire. "Well, if we ever meet, I'll kiss her on both cheeks and thank her."

"For what?"

She giggled, staring into the fire. "For being foolish enough to walk away from the finest catch in Kent County."

"I have a feeling that next time we come, you'll be walking on your own," Katie said cheerfully as she pushed Freeman's wheelchair out the automatic doors of the large medical complex. The visit had gone smoothly and much quicker than she'd expected. Not only did Freeman have a new, smaller and lighter cast, but he had permission to start walking.

An English child holding an adult's hand stopped and pointed at them, and the embarrassed mother tugged the little girl's hand. "Mama, look at the cowboy. He has a boo-boo."

"Sorry," the red-faced woman said. And then to her daughter, "Didn't I tell you not to talk to strangers?"

"But I wasn't," the child protested. "I just said—"

Katie glanced down at Freeman and pressed her lips together to keep from giggling out loud. He grinned back at her. "A cowboy?" she whispered.

He shrugged. "I've been called worse."

Chuckling, Katie pushed him down the sidewalk to a bench where the driver would pick them up. The clock in the doctor's office had told her that they'd have to wait fifteen minutes, but she didn't mind. The bench was in the shade, and she was content to be with Freeman.

Making sure he was in the shade, too, she sat down beside him. "I gave Isaac money and asked him to buy tickets for us for the Millers' spaghetti supper Friday night. The Ray Millers. They live out on Route 8. It's a benefit for the

Troyer baby who's up at the DuPont Children's Hospital. Isaac and Patsy are going to the benefit, and they said they'd be happy to come by and pick us both up and take us home afterwards."

Freeman's brow furrowed. "A benefit supper? I don't mind the donation, but I'm not sure I'm ready to go out in public. Not to something like that." He turned to her. "I wish you'd asked me about it first."

"Nonsense," she said, brushing off his protests. "It will do you good; maybe you can try your crutches. And it will certainly help the Troyers."

Freeman frowned. "I would have liked the chance to make up my own mind if I wanted to go before you committed us to having your brother go out of his way to take us."

"Fine." She folded her hands on her lap and watched a minivan go by. "If you don't feel up to it, I'll go by myself. I go to things like this by myself all the time."

"That's not the point, Katie. A man likes to be asked. Susan never—"

"Susan?" She turned to him. "Your old girlfriend's involved in whether or not we go out to a benefit supper?" She gave an exasperated sigh. "I don't know what to say. I thought you'd welcome the opportunity to go out and be with people."

He ran his hand over the new cast. "Maybe I would have, but now I feel as if I'm being told what I should and shouldn't do."

"I'm sorry, Freeman." She raised her hands and let them fall. "You're right. I should have asked you first. I'll tell Isaac that we've changed our minds and—"

"*Ne*. I'll go, but next time—ask me."

"I will," she agreed, somewhat chastened. She didn't know why he'd taken it wrong, but she'd have to tread more carefully, she supposed. She smiled at him, ready to move away from any unpleasantness. Not that she was concerned. This was the way two people got to know each other. "I'm so pleased that your recovery is coming along so well. In no time at all, you'll be dressing those millstones single-handedly."

"I sure hope so, because I've had enough of this thing." He tapped the wheelchair. "That looks like our driver coming now." He indicated a blue van that had just turned into the parking lot. "We can stop at the medical supplies place and pick up my new crutches, and then I have a surprise for you."

"A surprise?" She smiled at him. "What is it?"

He smiled at her. "I'm taking you to Rita's for a gelato."

"A what?"

"A gelato. It's kind of an ice cream and Icee all in one," he explained. "Have you ever had it before?"

"Never, but I love ice cream."

"Wait until you taste this. You'll be wanting me to take you every day for another."

Freeman frowned with concentration as he took another half dozen steps and stopped to lean more heavily on his crutches. He was breathing hard, and he still felt a little unsteady. "This isn't as easy as it looks," he said to Katie.

"It doesn't look easy." She stood beside him. "Maybe you've walked enough for one day."

"*Ne.* I need to build up my strength." He couldn't believe how weak he'd gotten in such a short time. His lips tightened into a thin line as he walked through the parlor and out onto the open front porch. Sweat beaded on his forehead, but he was pleased with himself. By the next week he'd be back in the mill putting in a few hours each day. He might not be ready for lifting, but there was nothing wrong with his mind. He could direct Shad, answer the telephone and wait on customers. His only regret was that more time in the mill would mean less time in the house. He'd loved the time with Katie every day, but he needed to get back to work.

Freeman took another step. Then another.

"Don't wear yourself out," Katie said as she followed him out onto the porch.

"I won't." The benefit spaghetti supper that had almost caused their first argument was that night. The thought that she hadn't consulted him before making arrangements for them to go with Isaac and Patsy still rubbed him the wrong way, but he'd given in, and that was the end of it. It wasn't worth getting upset about a second time. It was just something they were going to have to work on.

He lowered himself gingerly onto a high-backed wooden bench, and rested the crutches against his cast. Then he patted the space beside him and she took a seat. She was all in russet today, russet dress and scarf, and russet apron. He smiled at her. "I was thinking that maybe we could get a swing for out here. Maybe some chairs and a little table. Peachy has some solid outdoor furniture at a decent price. Unless you'd rather have new furniture in one room in the house. Maybe a new couch and chair in the parlor?"

She gave him a mischievous smile and curled her legs, tucking her bare feet under her. "I'm not sure that is a question you should be asking me. That's more for a husband and wife to decide, don't you think?"

"Once we're married, we *will* be husband and wife," he answered. "My furniture in the parlor belonged to my parents—you might rather pick something out yourself."

Katie rested two slender fingers against her lips. They were perfectly shaped lips to his way of thinking. Her lips had a natural peach tint that added to her attractive features. Katie was a looker. That was for sure.

"Freeman, aren't you getting ahead of yourself? When did we start officially courting?"

He liked the way her blond hair curled in little ringlets around her sweet face, but best of all, he liked her eyes, never dull, always sparkling, lively and full of swirling depths. With eyes like Katie's, a man would always be guessing what she was up to. He'd never be bored.

He chuckled. "When did we start courting? I thought we talked about this the other night at your brother's. Obviously we're courting. We started courting about five minutes after I got the nerve to ask you that day in the mill."

"But at the mill that day you said it was a *trial* courting." He could tell that she was trying not to smile, but she couldn't help herself.

"I know what I said, but…" He stopped and

started again. "But whatever I said that day, I'm saying now that we're courting, Katie Byler. And I intend to marry." He nodded, giving finality to his statement,

"Okay, then. We're courting. Officially now." She laughed and reached for his hand. Turning it over, she ran a finger over the calluses on his palm. "You have good hands," she murmured. "Hands tell a lot about a man."

"Do they now?" He didn't pull his hand away. He liked this playfulness in Katie. He liked sitting like this together. It made him happy to think that soon they could do it every day if they chose. They both were hard workers, but a man and his wife should take time for each other, to his way of thinking. Katie was easy to be with. She knew when to talk and when to sit quiet. It was one thing that he and Susan had always bumped heads on. While she never made assumptions and never disagreed with anything he said, she always had to be chattering away about this or that and sometimes he just wanted a little quiet. There were times when silence brought a couple closer than words.

She curled his hand into a gentle fist and released it. "Ivy's taking the buggy and going to Byler's to buy groceries to take over to the Marvin Kings. You heard they have his sister and her five children staying with them. They're the ones whose house burned last month."

He nodded, gazing out into the yard. Since Katie had come into his life, he had to admit the place looked better. The flowerbeds were weeded, the lawn was cut and she'd even painted the rails on the porch. "Jehu said the church districts are planning a house raising for them at the end of the month. The husband works construction, and he's been away. He burned his hands trying to save things from the house, and he missed a few weeks of work."

"The King place is small," she said, "and they have the daughter with cerebral palsy, as well as four other little ones. I'm sure they can use the extra groceries."

"We'll get them back on their feet again, both families. Our elders have taken up a collection for propane appliances for the new house. And the Seven Poplars community is providing the plumbing and bathroom fixtures for two full baths and the kitchen. Your Sara is donating a freezer and two sides of beef."

"I didn't know," Katie said. "Sara does a lot of good and never says a word about it."

"I wouldn't have known if my grandmother hadn't overheard Preacher Dan mention it to our bishop last church Sunday." He thought about his grandmother driving to Byler's Store and then on to the Kings' by herself. "Maybe Uncle Jehu should go with her," he suggested. "Just to keep her company." He nodded. "He's been sitting on the back porch since our noon meal, cat-cradling."

Katie shook her head. "Not cat-cradling, I don't think. He's learning to knit. I told him if he likes playing with yarn so much, to get Ivy to teach him to knit. Then he could make mittens for the school kids and scarves for the elderly. He liked the idea and Ivy was tickled to give him some instruction. I think it worries him that he can't contribute more."

*"Ya,"* Freeman agreed. "A difficult thing for a man to lose his eyesight. God's ways are sometimes hard to understand."

"And harder to accept with grace," Katie agreed. "Yet, we must. None of us can know His plan. We must rejoice in the blessings and endure the losses. But your uncle is a wise man. He has much to give to the community, especially to the younger people. He's a fine example of what a man should be."

"Exactly why he should go with Grossmama rather than let her go alone," Freeman said. He thought for a moment. "She hasn't left yet for the Kings' yet, has she?"

Katie shook her head. "I don't think so. Why?"

"I was just thinking, maybe she'd like some

company," he said, quickly warming to the idea. "And Uncle Jehu might want to go."

Just then Ivy appeared around the corner of the house. "There you are. I heard your voices. I'm leaving now. I'll be back before dark, but I don't know just when. Don't worry about me." She gave a wave. "I'm perfectly capable of driving a horse."

"I know you are, but be careful," Katie warned. "The traffic is busier on Fridays, especially Route 8."

"Don't worry," Ivy said. "I always take the back roads." She tightened the strings on her black bonnet that she wore over her prayer *kapp*. "Yoder Road is quiet. Not many cars."

Katie rose and walked to the porch railing. "Freeman thinks you should ask Jehu if he wants to come with you. Jehu and Marvin King go way back. It would be company for you, don't you think?"

Ivy's smile faded and suddenly she looked nervous. "Take Jehu? I don't imagine he'd want to go."

"You won't know unless you ask him," Freeman suggested. He could tell by his grandmother's expression that she wasn't opposed to the idea. In fact, he suspected, she liked it.

"I'll give it a try," Ivy said with a shrug. She

waved goodbye and disappeared around the end of the house again.

Freeman picked up his crutches and got shakily to his feet. "Think I'll take a stroll through the garden."

Determined, he made his way back through the house and down the ramp at the back porch. Uncle Jehu was no longer on the porch, although a pile of yarn and a tangle of something that might have been a scarf lay on the floor beside his chair. Katie followed Freeman down the walk and into the garden.

Going was a lot harder on the dirt, and they didn't stay long, just long enough to prove his point—that he could do it. As they exited the garden gate they heard the jingle of harness and the family buggy rattled past the house. Ivy was driving and his uncle was sitting beside her.

"Home later," Ivy called, happily.

"Don't hold supper!" Uncle Jehu hollered in their general direction. "We're getting subs at Byler's. Ivy and me."

"See," Katie said as she waved goodbye to them. Then she turned to Freeman. "You were right."

"You mean I had a good idea for a change?"

"Now, what's our next step?" Katie asked.

"Our next step?" He stopped to catch his breath.

She smiled the prettiest smile, his Katie. "To get them married, of course."

## Chapter Twelve

"You don't think that we're doing the wrong thing, interfering in Uncle Jehu and Grossmama's personal lives?" Freeman asked as he made his way gingerly up the ramp to his back porch.

Katie laughed. "Now's a fine time to wonder, isn't it? I think the deed is done." She stepped around him and held open the door, all the while bestowing on him an endearing smile that made him feel as happy inside as though he'd swallowed a glass of sunshine.

"I'm glad you're fully on board with the idea," she went on, her eyes twinkling. "I wouldn't be surprised if you aren't enjoying our success more than I am. You're good at this. Maybe you could give Sara a few pointers in the matchmaking game."

"It was your idea." He placed the first crutch

on the porch floor and took time to get his balance before putting his full weight on it. "I've known that my uncle is lonely, but I wasn't thinking about Grossmama. She's always been so independent—I didn't think she would want to marry again at her age."

"Maybe her age is exactly why she'd want to. Who wants to grow old alone if there's a special person who can fill the empty space in your home?"

"And heart?" he suggested. He settled into his chair and sighed with relief as he took the weight off his good leg. He felt a little lightheaded from the exercise, but he'd never admit it to Katie. He wanted her to see him as strong, able to protect her, not someone that needed to be cared for like a child.

"And heart," she agreed, taking the chair next to his and pulling it a little closer.

"I agree that it would be easier for me to have them settled, now that it looks like I'll be bringing a wife home this fall." He glanced at her. "If we call banns in September or October, we can marry in November after the crops are in. If you're agreeable."

"So soon?" she asked, wide-eyed. "I didn't think..." She looked down at her hands and then back up at him. "I assumed we would wait at least until spring."

"And why would we do that?" he asked her, realizing just how eager he was to marry her, now that his mind was made up. "We're of an age to know our own minds, aren't we? I know I'm past the time I should have married. And clearly, we're well suited." He met her gaze, resisting the urge to take her hand. They had both agreed they would be cautious with physical affection; there would be plenty of time for that after the wedding. "I don't want to rush you, but I don't see the need to drag out our courting any longer." He waited for her reaction, and when she just looked at him with doe eyes, he asked. "You do feel the same way, don't you, Katie?"

She lowered her head shyly. "*Ya*, I suppose, but you surprised me. It's all been so fast between us." Her cheeks took on a rosy hue and she nibbled on her lower lip. "I wouldn't want to make a mistake."

"You're the answer to my prayers. You could never be a mistake," he assured her. "And…" He waited until she raised her head and met his gaze straight on again. "I think it's time you broke the news to Kentucky Uriah. I feel like you've put it off long enough. It's not fair for him to think one thing when the truth is another." He tugged at the hem of her apron playfully. "I don't like thinking I've got competition."

"No competition. I already wrote to him."

She clasped her hands together in her lap. "I told him that I was walking out with someone here."

"Did you tell him you were betrothed?"

"I didn't because I'm not," she said.

He couldn't tell if she was teasing him or not. "I'm doing that now," he said firmly. "And it's not a *trial* betrothal. Can we set a wedding date for early November? That's the traditional month of marriage, when most of our guests will be free to attend. And I'd want a big wedding and that would give us time to choose our cooks and helpers and get out all the invitations. We can hold the service here, if you like. I want as many people as possible to share our happiness."

"Are you sure you don't want to wait a little longer before we decide?" she asked.

"I see no reason to wait. I won't change my mind. I want you for my wife."

"And I want you for my husband," she replied.

"So it's settled. I'll look at the calendar and speak to my bishop." He reached out and squeezed her hand, happier than he thought he'd ever been in his life. "And then you'll be mine."

On the following church Sunday, Katie accompanied Freeman, Ivy and Jehu to services at the Detweiler home. Once they arrived, Freeman and Uncle Jehu joined the group of men standing in the barnyard, while the women went into the house to wait until it was time to be seated. There Katie found herself eagerly welcomed into the crowded kitchen as Ivy introduced her to Viola, her hostess, and those women, girls and children of the worship community that she hadn't met before.

Each Amish church district made up their own larger family, worshiping and sharing the daily patterns of their lives, supporting those who needed help and taking pleasure in each other's company. When an Amish woman married, she would naturally attend her husband's church and live by the rules set by the community and the elders, so it was important that whomever Freeman married fit in, heart and mind. Many of these people, young and old, male and female, would be an intimate part of her life for years to come. Naturally, Katie couldn't help wondering if they would like her and if she would feel at home among them.

Shortly after their arrival, the older male members of the community and male guests filed in and took their places on benches on one side of the room, followed by the older women and honored women visitors who sat on the opposite side. Next came the unmarried women and the teenagers. Men and women always sat separately but young children and infants were passed between the groups at their leisure. When all were seated, an older man, the *vorsinger* or song leader, began the first hymn in a slow falsetto. Everyone joined in, and the elders took their seats near the front of the large living room. The hymn was a long one with many verses, and at the closing, the congregation knelt for the opening prayer and then rose in unison for the Bible reading.

The second hymn was always the *Loblied*. Gradually, Katie felt at ease as the voices rose in the much-loved song. She'd grown up in another district, with different preachers and another bishop, but this service was familiar and comforting. She liked red-haired Preacher Dan, who Freeman and Ivy had spoken of so highly, and she enjoyed his sermon on faithfulness. From her seat between two unmarried girls, she could see Freeman sitting several rows ahead of her on the far side. He'd been given a place by the aisle so that he could stretch out his leg and his crutches were under the bench. He couldn't see her without turning his head, and it pleased her to watch him without him being aware of it.

Morning service lasted nearly three hours, including the singing of hymns, Preacher Dan's sermon, a shorter sermon by the bishop, and the deacon's announcements of coming events and a planned day of fasting and silent prayer in sympathy for those caught up in foreign wars and displacement. Generations earlier, the Amish had been driven out of their homelands in Switzerland and Germany, many having suffered death and torture because of their religious beliefs. The bishop reminded them all that they must not forget that people today also suffered cruelly because of their faith in God. They might not be Amish, but it was the duty of the community to offer what help they could by remembering and praying for the victims.

The bishop's words touched Katie, and she went from the service to the communal dinner in a more serious state of mind than she had come in that morning. She'd rarely heard an Amish preacher or bishop urge his congregation to contemplate the plight of Englishers and consider their suffering. It was a good thing, she thought, a possible way to help, because she had a great belief in the power of prayer and in God's mercy. And it also brought back to each of them what sacrifices their own Amish forebearers had made so that they could find peace and a new home here in the United States of America.

After the closing hymn, everyone went outside where long tables had been set up for the traditional shared meal. Freeman was waiting for her near the corner of the house. "Are you doing okay?" he asked quietly, his expression anxious.

She nodded. "Of course, Freeman. I like your community."

"And is Grossmama looking after you? She promised me that she would."

"She is," Katie assured him. "Everyone is kind, and I like your Preacher Dan."

"Good. Good. Come, I want you to meet him and our bishop." Already nimble on his crutches, he led her over to where a group of the elders had gathered and introduced them. They exchanged a few pleasantries before Ivy came to ask her to assist in serving the food.

"Dinner," the bishop announced. He patted his ample stomach. "I like the sound of that." He smiled at her. "We are pleased to have you with us, and pleased that our friend Freeman has finally found someone he wants to spend his life with."

Katie flashed a shy smile at Freeman and then hurried away after Ivy, who explained to her that there had been a bit of a mishap in the kitchen involving two ornery little boys and a tray of sandwiches. The interior of the kitchen was a barely controlled chaos with crying babies and toddlers, giggling teenage girls whispering to each other, and Viola giving instructions. Katie saw the remains of the sandwiches scattered on the floor, found a broom and dustpan and quickly set about clearing the mess. The meat, cheese, lettuce and rolls on the table were being reassembled by an elderly white-haired woman in black and one of the girls, but what had fallen was obviously beyond saving, except as bounty for the chickens. Viola pointed the way to the poultry yard and Katie carried away the scraps.

Returning from the chicken house, she washed her hands and joined the other young women in transporting the meal to the first sitting, which consisted of the men and guests. The women and children would eat afterwards, partaking of the same food but with much less formality than was expected of those at first table. With the men fed, the women would be free to visit and eat at their leisure. And whatever cleanup chores were required, Ivy assured her that they wouldn't be expected to do it. Dish detail was regularly assigned to the teenage boys—quite a sensible arrangement, Katie thought.

Even with the loss of a great deal of the contents of the sandwich tray in the kitchen accident, there was more than enough food to feed everyone. As the men took their places at long tables under the trees in the yard, Viola put a pitcher of ice water into Katie's hands. "Emily's setting the glasses. Pour those who want water, then come back for the iced tea, then lemonade, then root beer."

"I have a better idea." Katie started uprighting glasses on a tray. "It will go quicker if we fill glasses here. Then we can each carry a tray with an assortment and ask everyone what they'd like to drink. It'll go faster that way."

"Well…I suppose…we could try it that way," Viola said, seeming flustered.

"Katie." Freeman called to her and motioned her over to where he was sitting.

"I'll be right back," she told Viola. Then to the other girls assigned drinks, she said, "Put the glasses on the trays and start pouring." She made her way to Freeman and bent her head to hear what he wanted to tell her.

"Must you be so…" He exhaled and started again, speaking under his breath. "Just do what Viola asked. No need to rearrange the process."

She straightened up, making a face at him. "But my way is so much easier. We'll be done in no time and people will have what they want to drink faster."

"Katie, you're new here. Best not to make a fuss," he whispered.

She took a breath before she responded. "So

what you're saying is that I should do it less efficiently so as not to make waves?"

He glanced at the men at the table, then back at her. "Please, Katie. Don't be difficult. You don't always have to be in charge."

"*Ne*, I suppose not." She could feel her cheeks burning. "I suppose Susan would not have done such a thing," she murmured. "I'm sure she knew her place."

"*Ya*," he said, obviously exasperated with her. "You're right there. Susan never made a fuss in public."

"I'm sure she didn't." Katie walked away, embarrassed, wanting desperately to have the last word, but too in control to make a complete fool of herself in front of Freeman's friends.

Once the drinks were poured and served, some in the manner Viola had instructed and some the way Katie had suggested, Katie returned to the kitchen. At the sink, she filled a dishpan of water and began to wash whatever she could find in the kitchen. Strictly speaking, washing dishes was work and work was not performed on the Sabbath, but most Amish women were too practical to fret over small sins and they cleaned up whatever came to hand when it was needed. Viola came in and began arranging casseroles on the counter, and Katie turned to her, dried her hands on a towel, and smiled. "It's so kind of you to have me in your home," she said.

"*Ya.* You are welcome here." Viola was brisk but not unfriendly.

"I hope I didn't speak out of turn. About the drinks. I didn't mean to cause a problem. I just get in a habit of doing things a certain way and…" She met her hostess's appraising look. "My mother tells me that I'm too forward. I ask your pardon if I offended you."

"For what?" Viola's lips curved up in a smile. "You were trying to help. And I've been called forward myself. I think we'll get on well enough, Katie Byler." She patted Katie's hand. "It's pleased I am that our Freeman has finally stopped moping over that Susan and looked around for a sensible young woman. I only hope that the two of you don't knock heads. You and Freeman, I mean. He's full of himself, but then most men are before they have a wife and children."

Katie chuckled.

"Now, if you wouldn't mind, there's another bucket of scraps for the chickens in the corner. I don't want fruit flies; you know what eager houseguests they can be." Viola, a thin bird of a woman with a snub nose and metal-rim glasses, pointed at a bucket on the floor. "Go out through the side door. It's quicker."

Katie picked up the bucket of garbage and went in the direction Viola sent her, down a hallway, through a utility room and side porch. She completed her task and was just hooking the door on the chicken house when Freeman came up the path, moving easily on his crutches.

"Katie. I was looking for you."

"So you found me." She realized her tone of voice was less than kind. She looked up at him, balanced on his crutches. He was getting stronger fast; soon he'd be able to put weight on the casted leg and would only need one crutch. She took a deep breath. "Freeman. Before you say anything, let me apologize." She set the bucket down. "I should never have said anything sarcastic about Susan. And you were right—I *was* too forward. I should have done what Viola asked, and I told her so. I'm sorry." She didn't want to argue with Freeman. She loved him. What was wrong with her that she spoke before thinking?

He shook his head. "I came to say that *I'm* sorry. I'm a dunce." He grimaced. "I should have kept my mouth shut and let you pass out drinks anyway you please. It was just that I wanted to make a good impression on my church family. And you did… I mean you have. There was no reason for me to worry; I should have known that. Viola likes you. She told me so. And several people came to me, just to say how happy they were with our betrothal announcement." He shrugged. "I suppose this is what comes of me not marrying younger. The older a man gets, the more convinced he is that he knows more than he does."

"A woman, too." She smiled up and him and he smiled back. She looked up to see his uncle approaching. "Uncle Jehu."

The older man came down the path at a steady pace, keeping to the center of the walkway with confidence. How did he do it? Katie wondered. Ivy had explained that Jehu could see light and dark shadows, but he certainly couldn't see the objects around him. "You never cease to amaze me," she said. "Are you part bat, that you can find your way without seeing?"

Jehu laughed merrily. "*Ne*, not that I've noticed. I just have a good memory."

"Uncle Jehu built this chicken house and the shed beside it," Freeman explained. "This used to be his farm."

*"Ach,"* Katie said. "I didn't know."

"And how would you?" Jehu asked her. He looked to his nephew. "There was something I wanted to talk to you about, if you have a minute. I was going to wait until tonight, but this seems as good a time as any."

Katie reached for the bucket. "I'll leave you two alone."

The older man shook his head. "No need. You've a sensible head on your shoulders, and I trust your judgment. I'd like your opinion, too, Katie." He took a deep breath and straightened his shoulders. "What would you say, Freeman, if I told you that I'd want your permission to walk out with Ivy?" He leaned in. "Am I a fool to think of marrying at my age?"

"Well, it's about time," Freeman replied enthusiastically. "Katie and I have been trying—"

Katie gave Freeman a hard tug on his arm, so hard, she was afraid she'd knocked him off balance and he was going to take a tumble. But it was enough to silence him. "Jehu! I think it's a wonderful idea," she said with enthusiasm. Freeman opened his mouth to speak again and she brought a finger to her lips, in an exaggerated motion. "I know how highly Ivy thinks of you."

"I hope so," Jehu said. "We've known one another for more than forty years, and I've always admired her. She knows my faults, and I've suffered her filling oat porridge for breakfast whether I wanted it or not." He looked up at Freeman. "I felt it right to ask for your blessing before I asked her if she'd be willing to court. Do I have it?"

Freeman grinned and nodded. "With all my heart, Uncle. You two are both dear to me, and I believe that marriage is something that would make you both happy."

"I think so, too," Uncle Jehu said. "I had a good marriage to a good woman, and I miss that companionship. It's not good for a man to be alone. Or a woman." He turned his head and smiled at Katie. "It seems you've come to the same conclusion."

"I knew it all along. It just took me a while to find the right girl," Freeman told him.

Uncle Jehu ran his fingers through his beard and tugged at the strands thoughtfully. "Well, the way I see it, there's no time like the present." He gave a wave. "No need to worry about us riding home with you in the buggy, following afternoon service. Ivy likes to walk home on Sundays when she can, and it's not far. It might do me a world of good to walk with her."

"Whatever you think best," Freeman agreed.

"I don't know about that." Uncle Jehu shook his head. "What I think best at the moment is for me to go back to the table and have a second piece of peach pie." He rubbed his midsection and chuckled. "But, common sense tells me I've eaten enough for one meal and need to leave enough for someone else." He gave a nod. "It heartens me that you two approve.

I'd not want to cause trouble under our roof or any other. But one thing I promise you, if your grandmother will have me, I'll do my best to care for her the way she deserves."

"I know you will," Freeman assured him as he walked away.

When they were alone again, she poked him in the side. "You weren't supposed to tell him it was our idea to see them together," she chided.

He pulled away from her, apparently ticklish. "I figured pretty quick that I said something wrong. You almost knocked me over."

She laughed with him. "Oh, I did not. A big strong man like you?" She dropped her hands to her hips. "It's best if he believes it was his idea to court your grandmother. Not that we'd come up with it and were trying to—"

"Manage their lives?" Freeman asked. He chuckled. "But we are, aren't we?"

"Maybe a little," she said, stepping in front of him to face him. "But with the best intentions."

"Thank goodness you stopped me," he told her. "I wouldn't want Uncle Jehu to think that I was trying to force him out of my house."

"He doesn't. He wouldn't. He knows what a good person you are."

Freeman leaned on his crutches and drew the tip of his index finger down her chin. "You think I am, Katie?"

Emotion constricted her throat. "I know you are," she murmured, looking into his warm eyes. "The best."

*"Goot."* He grinned at her. "Remember that when you're tempted to crack my knuckles with a spoon."

## Chapter Thirteen

From the mill's loading dock, Freeman waved as Preacher Dan drove out of the parking lot with six bags of chicken feed and two of hog chow in the back of his wagon just as the truck from R & W Stables was pulling into the lot. Freeman glanced at Shad. "Can you manage this order?"

Shad nodded. He removed his straw hat and used a handkerchief to wipe the sweat off his forehead. *"Ya."* A wide smile split his narrow face. "Bagged and waiting for'm. Same as last month and the one before."

"I'll leave you to it, then," Freeman pronounced. Loading the horse feed and mineral blocks was routine, but a task he wasn't quite ready for yet. He was off his crutches now. His doctor wanted him to put weight on the leg, but he needed the assistance of a cane, which wasn't exactly conducive to loading hundred-pound bags of feed.

Freeman eyed Shad. The young man might be a bit undersized for a miller, but he was strong for his size and he could move fast when he put his mind to it. Maybe he would prove his worth, as Katie and Uncle Jehu seemed to think. Shad's effort had improved by leaps and bounds in the last few weeks. Back at the start of summer, Freeman wouldn't have given him much of a chance of lasting until autumn, let alone keeping his job long enough to serve his apprenticeship. If it hadn't been for the accident, Freeman knew he probably would have sent Shad home to his mother and looked for a steadier employee. Katie's stubborn insistence that what Shad needed was more encouragement and more responsibility, rather than less, might have been what made the difference.

Freeman hated to admit it, but as an employer, he had a lot to learn. Maybe more than that, there was a great deal of wisdom he had to gain. Truth was, he had Katie to thank for saving his relationship with Shad. He would have lost a valuable asset because he hadn't been willing to try patience and trust. Katie was quite the woman, wise beyond her years. Hard to believe that he'd only really known her for a little more than eight weeks. Having her in his life had changed it so much for the better.

Using his cane, Freeman made his way down the ramp and toward the house. A fat mallard hen trailed after him, and following her, beak to bobbing tails were nine fluffy ducklings. "Go on back to the pond, *Mommi*," he said, waving his arm. "You're going to get your babies flattened in this parking lot." The duck paid no attention, so he dug in his pants pocket and came up with a handful of shelled corn. Using the food as bait, he led the ducks out of the lot, across the drive and down to the water's edge. He scattered the rest of the corn and then, while they were picking at the bright yellow kernels, he made his getaway.

Mingled peals of laughter from the yard drew his attention and he looked up to see his grandmother and uncle sitting side by side in a swing under the maple trees. Balls of multicolored wool were scattered all around their feet, and Grossmama was waving a length of knitting and giggling like a girl.

"What's so funny?" Freeman called.

"She's taunting a blind man," his uncle replied. "Just because my knitting is a little uneven."

"Uneven?" Grossmama doubled over with glee. "Freeman's tame crow could knit better with his beak tied behind him than this man. I wouldn't put this poor excuse for a baby blanket in a dog's bed."

"You see how she mistreats me," Uncle Jehu protested, pulling the little terrier into his lap and scratching behind the dog's ears.

His grandmother stood up and started picking up the stray balls of wool. "Pay no attention to him," she said. "There's none so blind as he who will not see."

Freeman looked from one to the other; they were obviously enjoying themselves. More importantly, each other. The two had been inseparable lately, so he supposed their courtship was going smoothly. Probably Katie could take credit for that blessing, as well. He couldn't remember when he'd seen Uncle Jehu smile more, and his grandmother now sang in the mornings when she worked in her flower garden. Maybe Uncle Jehu and Grossmama would have decided to court if Katie hadn't joined them, but there was no telling. They'd always been a family, but he had no doubts that Katie Byler had brought joy into this house and drawn them all closer.

Now that his leg had almost mended, Katie no longer came daily to help with the housework. Due to their ages and circumstances, Uncle Jehu and Grossmama might get around the rules. But it wasn't seemly that he and Katie, about to call their banns, should spend every day in each other's company. Nor did it seem right that she should be his housekeeper. It was the right decision but that didn't keep Freeman from missing her presence or from feeling that without her some of the light had gone out of his home.

Katie did come to visit his grandmother several times a week, and she was quick to lend him a hand where it was needed. Sometimes, she could be persuaded to walk down by the millpond with him, and several times he'd taken her out in the rowboat. They'd made the excuse that they were fishing, when really, it was a way to be alone together without crossing any unwritten rules of behavior for courting couples. They were in full view of anyone passing by, yet no one could approach them, and no one could overhear their conversation.

Once she stopped working for them, Katie hadn't returned to her brother's home, but had remained at Sara's. With the wedding so close, Katie had decided it would be better to leave his brother and new wife to themselves. Katie and Freeman continued to worship together on church Sundays and visit her family on the alternate Sabbaths. Twice, they had driven out in the evening to spend time with other young couples, but as much as he enjoyed the company of his friends, he found that he liked being alone with Katie best.

Freeman had never thought that he would talk to anyone the way he talked to her. She was a good listener, and she never held back when she had an opinion, but she was sensible. If he could defend his position and it was better than hers, she would come around without the least bit of resentment. Standing there seeing how Uncle Jehu and Grossmama were having such a good time together reminded him how much he and Katie found to laugh about. He'd often wondered if he'd ever find a woman that would fill the empty part in his life, and now, thanks be to the Lord God, he had. Katie Byler was the answer to his prayers.

They'd set a wedding date for the second Thursday in November, and they'd already picked their couples to attend them. The wedding couldn't come soon enough to suit him. Despite his earlier concerns about her strong personality and his determination that he be the master of his own house, Katie was his choice for a wife. He felt at odds without her beside him, and he expected his life to go smoother once the formalities were over and they could settle into married life.

As Freeman walked toward his grandmother

and uncle, he realized she must have been talking to him and he hadn't heard a word she said.

"Told you. You may as well talk to your knitting needles," Uncle Jehu said. "The boy's not heard a word you've said."

*"Ya,"* Freeman said. "Sorry. I was…"

His uncle laughed. "Woolgathering. Mind's on Katie, you can count on it."

"I'm sorry, Grossmama," Freeman said. "I'm listening now. What was it you said?"

"I said," she repeated merrily, "that Jehu and I were considering a day in October."

He blinked. "For?"

"We're doing no such thing," Uncle Jehu told her. Playfully, he flung a ball of wool in Ivy's direction. "We'll marry—*if* we marry—in December. We'll not be stealing the thunder from all you young rascals." He looked back at Freeman. "First we get you and Katie settled and then we'll see."

Freeman stared at her. "Married? The two of you have decided—"

"Sweet huckleberry buckle," his grandmother exclaimed, coming to her feet. "You can't think that we mean to waste the remainder of our days courting. Of course we're considering setting a wedding date."

Freeman caught her to him and hugged her.

"Congratulations. I think that's wonderful. Katie will be thrilled."

"Well, you're not to tell her yet, because we'll want to do that ourselves, once we speak to the bishop," Grossmama said. She kissed his cheek. "But you're a good boy. If I had a dozen grandsons, you'd still be my favorite."

"You know I'd do anything for you," Freeman said, releasing her and stepping back. "I'd be lost without you."

"The best thing you can do for her now," Uncle Jehu said, "is to marry that pretty girl of yours come November and give us a bevy of grandbabies to bounce on our knees."

"I'll marry Katie," Freeman promised. "As to the grandchildren, that's up to the Lord. You know we'll welcome as many as he chooses to send us."

"Amen to that," his grandmother whispered. "It's been far too long since we've had a new babe in this house." She beamed at Freeman. "But you cost me many a night's sleep. You were so set in your ways that I thought you'd end up an old bachelor with a house full of cats."

"Are you calling me hard to please?" Freeman asked.

"Truer words never spoken," Uncle Jehu chimed in. "Until sweet Katie came to us, we were both afraid that we'd be in our graves long before you ever found a woman you'd want to take to wife."

"I think that's it for this batch," Katie said as she turned off the heat under the pressure cooker. "We'll let it cool down and then put the last six quarts in." She and Ivy were in Freeman's kitchen, where they'd been canning tomatoes all morning. Two dozen pints and an equal number of quart jars stood on the windowsill. So far, every jar had been sealed. They looked wonderful and would taste even better when the temperature dropped and the cold winds of winter whipped around the farmhouse. Katie had always loved canning. It was hard work, usually in a sweltering kitchen in the first days of September, but the rewards were so great. It wasn't like sweeping the floor, where the results lasted only a few hours. There was nothing like pantry shelves filled with jars of fruit and vegetables to make a woman pleased with her efforts.

Ivy carefully ladled hot skinned tomatoes into waiting Mason jars. "It's so good of you to come and help me with this," she said. "And good of Sara to spare you."

"I'm glad to do it," Katie replied. "Canning is one job I never minded. And you've had such a bumper crop of tomatoes this year. It would be a shame to let any go to waste." She wiped down the jar rims with a clean dishtowel, added lids and screwed the rims into place. Then, using hot mitts, she lifted the filled jars and moved them to the counter beside the gas range.

Ivy finished filling the last jar and went to the sink to wash her hands. "Iced tea?" she asked.

Katie nodded. *"Danki."* Ivy made good tea, flavoring it with fresh mint leaves from her garden and using raw sugar instead of the white refined sugar that most people used. "I had a nice letter from Uriah yesterday," she said. "He said more in it than he ever has before. He seems like a good man. I hope he finds someone who will make him happy."

Ivy filled two glasses with ice and poured cold tea over top. "I know he must be sorry that you've chosen to wed someone else."

"He sounds as if he is." Katie glanced at her and smiled. "He says that if things don't work out, if I decide that I don't want to marry Freeman, he's still willing." She shrugged, amused that she'd gone years hoping for a husband and now she had more than one man willing to wed her.

Ivy chuckled. "Maybe you should think

again. This Uriah might have more sense than my grandson. Look at him." She pointed out the window. "Practically running across the yard, barely using his cane. I keep telling him not to get ahead of himself. Not to push himself too hard. Nobody can tell him anything. He always knows best." She shook her head. "He won't always be easy to live with, Katie. I warn you. I love him, but I know him all too well. God never made a more hardheaded man."

They heard the slam of the porch screen door. Ivy glanced up. "Don't bring that crow in here, Freeman. We're canning. We can't have feathers flying around while we're putting up food." She turned back to Katie. "You tell him, Katie. He won't listen to me. I don't want that crow in the house. Nasty bird."

Katie went to the kitchen door. Freeman did have the crow. It was riding on his shoulder. There was no cord on its leg. Apparently the crow sat there of its own volition. "Your grandmother wants you to leave the crow—" she began.

"I heard her," Freeman answered. "This crow's a lot cleaner than that dog of Uncle Jehu's, but she doesn't have to worry. I'm not bringing him in." He walked over to a hanging wooden bar that he'd suspended from the rafters in one corner of the porch and gently transferred the bird from his shoulder to the perch.

The bird settled, Freeman followed Katie into the kitchen. "That all you've got done?" he asked looking at the rows of cooling jars. "I know there's another half bushel basket of tomatoes outside. You think you'll get them all done today?"

Katie looked at Ivy and rolled her eyes. "Maybe we will and maybe we won't," she said. "Mind your own beeswax. If we don't finish today, I'll come back tomorrow."

Freeman wandered over to the stove, paying her no mind. "These finished?" he asked, indicating the pressure canner.

*"Ya,"* his grandmother replied. "Just waiting for the steam to die down."

Freeman set his cane against the counter and reached up to remove the weight from the top of the canner. "You've got to remove this to release the pressure," he explained, as if he thought neither of them had ever canned tomatoes before.

"Careful," Katie warned. "You'll burn your—"

"Ouch!" A hiss of steam came from the canner and Freeman jumped back, rubbing his thumb and forefinger together.

"You okay?" Katie asked, suppressing the urge to giggle. It wasn't nice to laugh at his pain, but how could he be so silly as to not know you didn't just remove the weight?

"Fine." He licked his injured finger.

"You need a cold cloth for that?"

"Nope," he told her.

"Then wash up and sit down at the table. We've got hot vegetable soup and ham sandwiches for nooning."

"Sandwiches?" he asked pitifully. "I hope you've made a stack of them. I'm starving."

"Canning days you're fortunate to get sandwiches," Ivy said. "When I was growing up, we made do with stewed tomatoes on bread when my mother was doing up vegetables." She looked around. "Where's Jehu? He's not usually late to table."

"In the garden," Freeman said. The tip of his finger was red and he went to the sink and ran cold water on it. "He said he wanted to pick the last ears of corn for you. No more fresh corn until next summer now."

Katie handed him a towel to dry his hand.

"I don't see salt," Freeman said, looking at the counter. "You didn't forget to put salt in the jars, did you? My mother always put a half a teaspoon of salt in every jar. To help seal it, I think."

Katie grimaced. "Salt makes the tomatoes salty, and we don't need to add salt when we don't have to. Especially not for your grand-mother or Uncle Jehu. Too much salt can cause high blood pressure. Strokes. We don't need salt to make the jars seal. That's an old wives' tale."

Freeman looked skeptical. "You always used salt, didn't you, Grossmama? I'm sure you're supposed to."

"Maybe I did and maybe I didn't," she said, taking a plate of sandwiches Katie had made earlier from the refrigerator. "But we decided not to do it this year."

"All the same, what does the canning book say?"

"Freeman, will you let it go?" Katie said. She wanted to swat him with a damp towel. "We know what we're doing. We don't need your advice on canning. This is women's business, not men's."

"I'm just trying to help," he protested.

"I know," she answered, trying not to let her annoyance with him show. "I know you are, but—"

"You have to admit, I've been right in the past. You asked me for advice, and I—"

"Might have needed it before," she said. "But not now. I've already caught a husband, haven't I? So I must not be doing everything wrong."

"Whoa. Whoa." He shook his head. "Sorry.

All I wanted to do was make a suggestion, but if you don't want it, that's fine."

The screen door banged again and Katie heard footsteps on the porch for a second time. "Uncle Jehu?"

"Got some corn," he replied. "I've husked it outside. Thought it might go good for lunch with the soup and sandwiches."

"Bring it in," Ivy ordered. "I'll put a pot of water on." She looked at Katie. "It won't take long to steam the corn."

"How long?" Freeman asked.

"Maybe five or ten minutes to heat the water. Another five to steam the corn," Katie said. "We can sit down and start on the sandwiches. The soup's almost heated."

"*Ne*, that's fine." He smiled at her. "I'd like you to see something. It will just take five minutes. If you wouldn't mind coming out to the mill while the corn cooks."

Katie looked back at Ivy.

"Go on, child. I can manage six ears of corn."

"We'll be right back," Freeman assured his grandmother.

Katie removed her soiled apron and hung it over a chair, then followed him out of the house and across to the mill. "What are we going to see?" she asked, tickled to have a few minutes alone with him. She'd been sad when he insisted she couldn't work as his housekeeper anymore; she missed him on the days she didn't get to see him. But when they did see each other, Freeman was good at making sure they were always able to steal a few minutes alone.

"It's a surprise," he said. He'd left his cane in the kitchen, so he linked his arm through hers. If anyone saw them, she knew he could make the argument she was assisting, but she knew better. He liked this innocent physical contact as much as she did.

"It's for you. For us." He led her across the yard and into the back section of the mill, an area that she'd never seen before. "I've got a workshop back here," he explained. "And there's something here for you." He opened a back door and motioned to her. "See what you think of this."

She paused, letting her eyes adjust to the dimmer light inside the building. Standing in the center of a large room was a dark oak dresser and a bed with a tall carved headboard and turned foot posts. "Oh," she breathed as she approached the bed and ran a hand over the nearest post. Carved into the headboard and posts were tulips and a pattern of vines. The craftsmanship was lovely, the tulips stained red and the vines green. "You made this for me?" she asked. Tears clouded her vision. "Freeman…

I don't know what to say." It was so sweet of him. The intricate flower pattern wasn't really her taste, but she would have glued her mouth shut before she would have ever admitted it. If Freeman thought this was beautiful, then she would learn to love it as she loved him.

"*Ne*. I didn't make them." Freeman shook his head. He walked to the tall dresser and pointed out the same tulip-and-vine pattern on the front of the drawers. "A Mennonite fellow down in Greenwood makes these. I just remembered they were here. Susan and I saw them at the state fair and I had him make them for—"

"You had the set made for Susan?" she interrupted, feeling as if she were the pressure cooker on the stove. She was suddenly so angry that she thought steam might come out of her ears.

Freeman didn't seem to notice. He looked so pleased with himself. "*Ya*. I never gave them to her, of course. It was supposed to be a wedding gift. She saw it and liked it and I ordered it. But by the time the cabinetmaker finished them, Susan and I had already parted ways. It's been sitting here all these years. I pulled the canvas off and polished them up. What do you think?" He leaned against the doorframe. "Pretty, aren't they?"

She turned to him, planting her hands on her

hips. She didn't know if she wanted to holler at him or cry. She felt as if suddenly the ground beneath her was shifting. How could she have been so mistaken? How had she not seen this before? "You think I want to sleep in a bed you bought for another woman?" she demanded.

Freeman stared at her in obvious confusion. "Why not? It's brand-new. Nobody ever slept in it. I thought you'd like it."

"But you bought it for her." Her voice didn't sound like her own. "For Susan."

He frowned. "What difference does it make who I bought it for? It's an expensive bedroom set. I thought that you—"

"You thought wrong!"

He drew himself up. "No need to get huffy with me. Most women would—"

"You bought it for Susan," she interrupted. "I'd sleep on the floor before I'd sleep in her bed. In what she picked out."

"That's the dumbest thing I've ever heard, Katie."

Katie backed away. At first she was angry. Now she was hurt. So hurt. She could feel tears burning her eyes. "Am I always to be second place to her, Freeman? To Susan? Is it me you love and want to marry? Or is it still Susan? Are you still in love with her?"

He scowled as if that were the most ridiculous thing a person had ever said to him. "*Ne*! Of course not."

"But you *wish* I was more like her." She walked past him, out into the humid day. Away from the pretty bed and dresser that weren't really hers. That would never be hers. "Tell the truth, Freeman. You do wish I was Susan, don't you?"

"Sometimes, maybe I do," he blurted. "At least she wasn't a shrew. Susan would have had the good manners never to throw a gift back into a man's face."

"But I'm *not* Susan. I'm going to say what I think. You know that about me. And I'm never going to be the biddable wife you want."

"You're being hysterical." He waved his hand. "Blowing this all out of proportion."

"Am I?" She shook her head. "I don't think so. This just shows how little you know me. How little you understand about who I am."

"Katie, don't make more of this than it is. If you don't like the bedroom set, fine." He threw up his hand. "We can sell it."

"There's no need." She wanted to turn and walk away. Run. But she held her ground, looking up at him. His face was flushed and she could tell he was angry, too. "Keep it and give it to the next girl you court."

"Katie. Listen to reason."

"I am," she flung, tears running down her face. "And reason tells me that I can't marry you. Find someone else," she cried. "Someone who will say 'yes, Freeman, of course Freeman,' like Susan. Because I can't do that. I won't."

His eyes narrowed. She could see his shoulders tense and feel the anger emanating from him. "If that's the way you feel," he said, "then so be it. Better to end it now before any more harm is done."

"You're right," she answered hotly. "Before anyone's heart is broken."

# Chapter Fourteen

Katie knocked on the partially open door of Sara's sewing room. She'd been awake most of the night, and had alternated her hours between pacing the floor and praying on her knees. The prayer might have helped; the walking hadn't. And now that she'd come to a decision, she felt that she had to confide in Sara before doing anything else.

"Yes?"

Katie pushed open the door and stood in the doorway.

The dark-eyed matchmaker looked up from the treadle Singer sewing machine and smiled. "I was wondering where you got to this morning." Sara gathered the olive-green skirt she'd been stitching and held it up. "What do you think of this fabric? I'm making a new dress for one of Wayne Lapp's girls. It's a lovely blend.

It should wash well and come off the line without a lot of wrinkles."

"It's lovely," Katie said. The Lapps had a houseful of children and a limited income. Sara was a master seamstress, and a new dress would be welcome and could be handed down to smaller sisters when the recipient had outgrown it.

"Well, don't just stand there. Come in." Sara waved her in.

This was one of Katie's favorite rooms in the house—Sara's sewing room. A battered old pine table held cut and pinned lengths of cloth that, once stitched together, looked like a black Sunday dress for someone. Katie tried to compose herself as she took in the pleasant room. Nearly square, it was painted a restful pale blue with two large windows, a colorful rag rug, and two rocking chairs placed side by side to catch the light. One wall boasted an oversized maple cabinet rescued from a twentieth-century millinery shop and open drawers revealed an assortment of various sizes of thread, needles, scissors and paper patterns. A small walnut table with turned legs stood between the windows and held a cheerful bouquet of yellow zinnias and blue cornflowers. Sara loved fresh flowers and she placed them throughout her home. It was a practice that

Katie wanted to emulate when and if she ever had her own house.

Sara studied Katie's face. "Why do I get the idea that something has gone very wrong for you?"

Katie was afraid she was going to burst into tears. She still couldn't believe what had seemed so good between her and Freeman had turned out so badly, so quickly. "I need to talk to you." She swallowed, trying to regain her composure.

Sara nodded. "Of course. When you didn't take supper with us last night, and then didn't come down to breakfast, I guessed that you were upset." She rose from her chair at the sewing machine and motioned toward the rockers. "Will you sit?"

Katie rubbed her hands nervously on her apron. "*Ne*. What I have to say won't take long." She looked at Sara with what she knew were puffy and probably red and swollen eyes. She'd cried last night, but she was done weeping, and she hoped she could carry on without making a fool of herself. "I've broken off my betrothal to Freeman," she said quietly. "It's over between us."

"Oh, Katie." Sara brought fingertips to her lips in a sigh. "Why? Did you argue?"

"We did."

"That happens with every couple." Sara looked down and then back up at Katie. "Are you sure this isn't something that can be smoothed over? A lovers' quarrel?"

Katie shook her head. "*Ne*. I wish it was, but this can't be fixed."

Again, Sara hesitated. "I'm so sorry. I was so sure that the two of you were a solid match." Her eyes filled with compassion. "I believed that you were right for each other, that you were in love."

"I was in love with him," Katie assured her. "Maybe I always will be, but loving someone doesn't mean that you'd be a good wife for him." She caught the hem of her apron, balling it in her fist. "I can't marry Freeman, because he still cares for the woman that he almost married ten years ago. She's been a shadow between us from the beginning. I should have seen it sooner. And... I can never measure up to her memory. I realized yesterday that I couldn't marry him, knowing he loves her."

Sara exhaled loudly, sounding impatient now. "You two. You're like a pair of goats knocking heads. I knew you were both strong-willed, but sometimes that works best in a marriage. One balances out the other. You and Freeman are alike in so many ways. Is it possible that you misinterpreted his—"

"*Ne.*" Katie shook her head. "There's no mistake. He brings her up all the time. He compares us. All the time. I can't live that way. Not for the rest of my life."

They were both quiet for a minute.

"The decision is yours," Sara said softly. "But I have to advise you not to be hasty."

"I've made up my mind, Sara. I know I'm doing the right thing." As she said the words, she felt less sure of them, but she refused to second-guess herself.

"I hope you are." Sara's eyes crinkled at the corners. "Because Freeman seems such a sensible man. I find it hard to believe he'd still be mooning over a woman after ten years."

"Well, it's true." Katie put her hands together and intertwined her fingers. "I can't marry him knowing that he'd rather I was someone else. I won't try to compete with a ghost."

"A ghost?" Sara lifted a brow questioningly. "Is she dead?"

Katie shook her head. "Not dead. Married with a family of her own. But he remembers her as all the things I'm not. *Sweet Susan. Meek Susan.* A woman who knew when to give way to a man's will. Biddable, that's what he called her. And that's what I'm not."

Sara approached and took both of Katie's

hands in hers. "Please reconsider. It's easy to make decisions in anger."

"He took me out to the mill to show me a *surprise*. He's kept the bedroom set he bought for her. He thought it would be our wedding bed. Can you imagine? Susan's bed? I couldn't sleep a night in it." A tear trickled down Katie's cheek and she dashed it away with the back of her hand. "He doesn't need someone like me, Sara. He needs someone who will say yes to every notion he has. We'd never be happy together." She sniffed.

Sara plucked a handkerchief from her pocket and handed it to her. "Blow your nose. Dry your eyes. This isn't the first argument that an engaged couple has had. As I said—"

"I value your advice, Sara," Katie said firmly, "but I can't go through with this knowing what I know. It wouldn't be fair to either of us."

"I can understand why you're so upset, but you have to remember, men often don't have a clue as to how women think. And if we women are honest about it, we're not always so good about telling our men what's going on in our hearts or our heads." Sara sighed. "I've been matching couples for a long time, and yours was one I felt certain would be successful."

"I'm sorry to disappoint you, then."

"Oh, Katie, you haven't disappointed me."

Eyes misty, Sara held out her arms and hugged Katie tightly when she moved into them. "I know you're hurt," Sara murmured. "I can see it in your eyes. All I'm saying is that I wish you would give it a few days before making up your mind that you can't find your way past this. Let me talk to him."

"*Ne*. I've made my mind up." Katie shook her head emphatically. "I spent the night wrestling with this, and my decision is final. I won't marry Freeman. And I won't sit around moping over it. I want to go to Kentucky to visit Uriah and his family. I think that marrying him would be best."

Sara frowned. Doubt flickered in her eyes. "Again, I have to counsel you against impulsiveness. If you and Freeman love each other, misunderstandings can be straightened out."

"*Ne*." Katie shook her head firmly. "I won't change my mind. If you'd been there, Sara, you'd understand." She folded her arms over her chest. "I think Freeman was relieved. He wouldn't have backed out of our engagement because he's not that kind of man, but I think he realized I was right. We're not suited." She let her hands fall to her sides. "So if Uriah still wants me, and if he doesn't have two heads or something terrible, then I'll marry him."

"I can't help thinking that you're making a

mistake," Sara said. "At the least, you should wait a decent time before considering Uriah's offer."

"Aren't you the one who told me that marriages are made in heaven?" Katie raised her chin stubbornly. She knew Sara was going to try to talk her out of this, but she'd already decided she wouldn't be swayed. "If Uriah and I have respect for each other, if we marry to make a new family, we can learn to love each other. It's better that way. No foolish delusions of love between us, but the opportunity to form a strong union, one where we can raise our children in the faith."

Sara looked troubled. "As your friend, I recommend you wait a few days, or better still a few weeks. This may look differently in time."

"If I wait, I'll lose my nerve," Katie insisted. "I should have accepted Uriah's offer months ago. I'm going to walk over to the chair shop this minute and call Uriah's father's harness shop. His sister has invited me to come and stay with her. And I'm going."

"Decisions made in haste are often repented in leisure," Sara told her. "Once Freeman has a chance to think about the mistake he's made, then maybe the two of you can see your way through this."

"I told you, Sara. I'm through with Freeman."

She walked to the door, eager to be out and on her way. The sooner she made the phone call, the sooner she'd be headed for her new life. "I'm going to Kentucky as quickly as I can make the arrangements. I know what I'm doing, and I know what will make me happy in the long run. Falling in love with Freeman was a mistake. And the best thing I can do is to move on with my life and forget him."

Freeman dumped a scoop of horse feed into the donkey's outdoor feed bin in the corral and watched as the aging animal ambled over. Business was slow at the mill this morning, and he could find nothing to occupy his mind. His leg ached. The doctor said that it was healing fast, but that he had to expect a little discomfort in the process. Freeman leaned over the rail and stroked the back of the gray donkey that had a darker gray mark across his shoulders. The animal wiggled his ears and munched at the grain.

"Look at you," Freeman said. "Not a care in the world." The donkey just kept eating. The crow Freeman and Katie had rescued hopped across the grass and came to rest a few yards from where Freeman stood. It opened its mouth and let out a raucous caw. Freeman dug in his trouser pocket and found a crumpled biscuit from breakfast. He tossed a piece to the crow and the bird gobbled it and croaked again, wanting more. Freeman threw the rest of the bread, picked up the grain scoop and walked back toward the house, using his cane for support on the uneven ground. He'd put the grain scoop away on his next trip to the barn.

It was a fair day, not too hot, and slightly overcast, with a light breeze. Autumn was coming, his favorite time of year. Ordinarily, Freeman would have rejoiced in the break from the late summer heat, but today nothing pleased him. The crow made a few hops as if to follow him and then flew up to the top of a fence post and perched there, beady black eyes staring at him.

"That's it," Freeman said. "Nothing more. You'll be so fat you won't be able to fly." The bird had made an amazing recovery once the broken leg was splinted.

"Stray animals, it's all I'll have," Freeman muttered under his breath. "Cats, crows and useless donkeys." It was probably for the best that he and Katie had parted ways when they had. He wasn't cut out for marriage. He was meant for the bachelor life. No matter how hard he tried to make it work with a woman, it ended badly. Shouldn't a man know when it was time to give up on a bad idea?

Over the last twenty-four hours Freeman had

gone over and over his and Katie's parting argument, and he couldn't see where he'd put a foot wrong. He'd honestly expected her to be pleased with the bedroom suite. It was brand-new and it wasn't as if Susan had ever slept in the bed. It made no sense. What kind of man did she think he was? If he still had feelings for Susan, he certainly wouldn't have entered into a courtship with Katie. It hurt him that she thought he was that man. And the fact that she didn't know him better than that made him wonder if he really knew her. He exhaled, too worn-out to keep going over it all in his head. Maybe this was all for the best. Maybe it was good to learn her character now rather than later when it was too late to back out of a bad marriage.

"Freeman!"

His grandmother and Uncle Jehu were just coming out of the garden, each carrying a bushel basket of lima beans. Freeman crossed the distance to where they stood near the gate, passed her the metal scoop, and took the heavy basket. Even though he was still using the cane to walk, he was finding he could carry quite a bit of weight. "I'll carry these back to the house for you," he offered.

"You can help us shell them, too," his uncle

said. "No sense wasting your day lazing around feeling sorry for yourself."

"That what you think I'm doing?" Freeman asked. It was a barb that hit too close to home. He couldn't stop thinking about Katie and wondering how their happiness could have ended so quickly. She'd been wrong to take offense about the bedroom suite, and she'd been mistaken when she accused him of still being in love with Susan. How did things get so confused between them? His worries about Katie had never been that he wanted her to be someone else. Rather, he'd been afraid that he wasn't strong enough for such a woman. A man should be the head of his house. He didn't want to end up like his parents, with the wife's word being what counted. After knowing Katie, he could see that someone like Susan would have been all wrong for him. Susan was too meek, too unwilling to give an opinion or an idea.

"It's plain that you argued," Uncle Jehu said. "You may as well tell us what you argued over."

"I don't see that that'll be of any use to anyone."

"Come on. You may as well tell us," Grossmama said. "You know I'll have it out of you before the day is over."

Unwillingly, feeling like a boy who'd done something wrong and been caught in his mischief, he explained about the bed. And, as he expected, which was why he hadn't told them what happened in the first place, he got no sympathy.

"Ridiculous," his uncle declared. "What ever possessed you to think that Susan's bedroom suite would please Katie?"

"I agree," his grandmother said. "You were completely in the wrong."

"Wait a minute. You weren't there," he defended. "You didn't hear what she said to me."

"Nonsense," Grossmama replied. "She's as bad as you are. Such impulsive behavior out of two grown people who love each other." She shook her head. "You're unhappy without her, and if you don't come to your senses, you'll be unhappy for the rest of your life."

Freeman clenched his teeth together. He would never be disrespectful to his grandmother, but she was wrong to interfere in his affairs. She didn't understand why he couldn't allow Katie to have her way.

"Listen to her," Uncle Jehu said. "You're making a big mistake. Ivy's telling you the honest truth. You'll never meet another woman like Katie, and you're a fool if you let her go."

"You two don't understand," Freeman protested. "I'm not my father. I can't be ruled by a woman the way he was ruled by my mother."

"Ah, so is that what the trouble is? You think your mother made your father unhappy and you don't want to see yourself in the same fix?" Grossmama asked. She headed for the house and Freeman had no choice but to follow. "He loved her," she went on. "He let her do and say what she wanted until it was something he cared about. And then it was his will that won out. Your father was a good man, Freeman, but he wasn't a forceful man. He was my son, my only child. No one knows him as I did. He used to say that your mother saved him a lot of worry by making small decisions. It left him free to make the big ones. It was the way their marriage worked. No one can judge whether what they did was always the best, but it was their choice to make. And if you've rejected Katie because of something you believe made your father less than he was, you're dead wrong."

"You're a man grown," Uncle Jehu insisted, walking on the other side of Freeman so that he was caught between the two of them. "Not a foolish boy. And men and women work out their differences. You don't turn your back on each other." He stopped and set his basket of pole limas on the ground and pointed a finger in Freeman's direction. "If you love her, you should be man enough to do what it takes to settle this nonsense. Of course, if it was just a marriage of convenience—"

"You know that it wasn't," Freeman said softly.

"Then admit that you were wrong," his grandmother said. "If you'd told me you meant to give her Susan's furniture, I could have told you that it was a crazy scheme. I'd have told you Katie wouldn't go for it, and I have to say, I wouldn't either." She gestured. "Sell the set or give it to Jehu and me for a wedding gift. We'll be needing a marriage bed, and I always liked those tulips. Cheerful, they are."

"She's right," Uncle Jehu chimed in. "A woman wants to pick out her own furniture. I've got a fine bed that suited me and my wife for a lot of years, but I wouldn't think to bring a new wife to it." He shook his head, making a clicking sound between his teeth. "For a smart boy, Freeman, you sometimes set me to wondering if your brains are made of wood."

"I think it's too late. Katie and I both said things that shouldn't have been said," Freeman explained. "I don't know if we can take back those angry words."

"Of course you can. The Bible tells us to forgive," his uncle said as he took Ivy's hand in his. "And not just others, but ourselves. We're human and we make mistakes, but a smart man doesn't let a mistake bring him to his knees. Pride and hurt feelings don't mean much compared to a future without the woman who makes up your other half."

Freeman looked from one to the other and then down at the grass at his feet. He tapped at a weed with his cane. "You think I made a mistake in letting her go?"

"What do *you* think?"

He stared at the ground. "I think…I think I love her and—" his voice cracked "—I think I'll never be happy without her." He looked up at his grandmother. "You really think I made a mistake in letting her go?"

"Are you slow-witted, grandson?" Grossmama demanded. "Haven't we just said that?" She pursed her lips. "Now, what are you going to do to make it right?"

The distance from the mill to Sara Yoder's house wasn't far, but it seemed to Freeman to take forever for the horse to cover the miles. Now that he looked at his argument with Katie from another direction and had time to think it over, he couldn't see how they'd let the problem divide them. He didn't know how *he* had let their misunderstanding go so far. He'd been angry that she accused him of still loving Susan and he hadn't been willing to listen to her side.

Katie might have been equally to blame, but that didn't matter. He'd let two whole days and nights pass without reaching out to her. That had been his second mistake, and the sickness in his belly proved that nothing would be right until they mended this disagreement.

He shook the reins over the horse's rump. "Get up!" he cried, relieved he could drive again. The animal picked up speed. The wheels of the buggy clattered on the hardtop road, and the farmland on either side of the road sped by.

He was moving so fast that when he turned the horse into Sara's drive, the buggy went up on two wheels before righting itself and bouncing into place. Freeman's pulse quickened. He wasn't sure what he'd say to Katie when he came face to face with her, but he'd think of something. They belonged together, and if he had to light a match to Susan's bed to prove to Katie that he put her first, then that was what he'd do.

When he reined the horse up short near Sara's back door, he saw the matchmaker sweeping the porch. "Sara!" he called. "Is Katie here? I have to talk to her."

Sara leaned her broom against a post and came down the steps.

"It's nothing we can't settle," he went on. "Just a misunderstanding with two hotheads facing toe-to-toe." He looked around, hoping that Katie had heard the horse and buggy drive into the yard, hoping that she would come out of the house.

Sara looked up at him. "Freeman," she said gently. "Katie's gone."

He felt a sudden heaviness in the pit of his stomach and went lightheaded. "Gone where?"

Sara's voice was thick with emotion. "I'm so sorry. I tried to talk her out of it, but you know how she gets. Freeman, she's gone to Kentucky."

"Just like that?" He looked away; his eyes were burning.

"I tried to convince her not to make any decisions while she was so upset. I told her she was being impulsive."

"I did something stupid. Katie misunderstood, and we ended up arguing. It was all my fault. But I came to make things right, to ask her to forgive me." He looked down at Sara, standing beside his buggy. "She can't be gone."

"Do you love her?"

"With all my heart."

Sara considered him for a moment, then reached up and rested her hand on his forearm. "Then you have to go after her, Freeman. You have to stop her before it's too late." Her round face was taut with concern. "Because I think she means to marry Uriah as soon as the wedding can be arranged."

## Chapter Fifteen

"Can you go any faster?" Freeman demanded of the van driver. They were approaching the bridge over the Delaware and Chesapeake Canal on Route 1, headed toward the Amtrak Station in Wilmington. "We have to get there before the train leaves." Before Katie leaves for Kentucky, he thought anxiously.

"We have to get to the train station in one piece and without me getting a speeding ticket," Jerry Kaplan answered. Heavy raindrops beat against the windshield and the wipers kept up a steady rhythm.

Freeman leaned forward, gripping the armrest. Jerry, a retired state trooper, was the fifth driver he'd called. The first four drivers who usually transported the Kent County Amish and whom he'd called were either busy or couldn't be persuaded to drive as far as Wilmington. Freeman had never hired Jerry before but Roman at the chair shop in Seven Poplars, where he'd made the phone calls, had recommended him. Jerry was a long-distance driver who also took passengers to the train station or to the Philadelphia or Baltimore airports in his big SUV.

"A lot of other motor vehicles are passing us," Freeman said. "They can't all be speeding, can they?" The front passenger's seat was pushed back so that his healing leg wasn't cramped, but Freeman couldn't appreciate the comfort. All he could think of was getting to Katie before it was too late—finding her and convincing her to give him a second chance.

"Most are," Jerry replied. He was a big man, balding, soft-spoken, and still physically fit, despite his seventy-one years. "And most of those who do pass us, we'll see again when we hit heavier traffic up ahead. We would have stood a better chance of catching up with your lady friend if we'd left an hour earlier." He glanced over at Freeman. "If you remember, I told you there were no guarantees."

"I know," he agreed. "You were honest with me. And I appreciate you taking the time to drive me. It's just that it's so important I reach her before the train pulls out."

Jerry Kaplan seemed a decent man and was

a good driver. He was certainly an honest one. Freeman had offered the retired policeman twice his normal fare to drive him to Wilmington and three times it if they got there in time to stop Katie from leaving. Jerry had refused the additional fee and declared that his usual charge was fair for them both.

Ordinarily, Freeman would have enjoyed talking with the Englisher. But he had no words or thoughts to spare for anyone but Katie. How could he have been such a thick-headed fool? Why had he been so quick to defend himself and so slow to see her side of the disagreement? Katie was the best thing that had ever happened to him and he might lose her forever because of his own stubborn desire to always have things his way.

He tapped his good foot impatiently as traffic ahead of them slowed to a near stop. Who was he to criticize Katie for willfulness? He was worse than she was because he'd experienced heartbreak before. He should have realized how special his and Katie's relationship was and fought to protect it.

Freeman felt a sick hollowness inside. All he wanted was the opportunity to speak to Katie before she got on that train to Kentucky. He was certain he could get her to reconsider.

If only Jerry could get him there on time.

When Sara told him that Katie had left for the train station, he'd felt as if he'd taken a blow to his midsection, and he still felt sick. He'd gone directly from Sara's house to the Seven Poplars chair shop to use the phone and call for a driver and check the train schedule. He'd left his horse with one of the young men there and asked him to get the animal home to the mill and tell his family where he'd gone.

For once, Freeman wished that the elders in his church approved of cell phones for their members' personal use. Englishers carried their phones everywhere. If both he and Katie had a cell phone, he wouldn't have to chase her down. They could've settled this misunderstanding with one call. But maybe talking to her by phone wouldn't have been enough. And maybe if he *did* get to her before her train pulled out, she'd still reject him.

And then what? He had no backup plan. The only thing he knew was that he loved Katie. He wanted her for his wife. And if he lost her, he'd never find happiness with another woman.

Freeman glanced at the clock on the dashboard. Seven minutes since he'd last checked the time. How far had they gone? And how much farther was the train station? "Please, God," he whispered under his breath. "I'll be a better man. I've learned my lesson. Let me get there before it's too late."

Jerry braked and pulled to the curb half a block from the train station. "It will be faster if you get out here. I'll park in the garage and find you inside," he said. "Good luck. I hope you find your lady friend."

Freeman was unbuckled and halfway out of the door before the SUV came to a complete stop. With the help of his cane he took the sidewalk toward the front entrance of the station. People carrying suitcases crowded the way, and a few glanced at him with curiosity. He didn't pay any attention. He barely avoided tripping over a baby stroller loaded with packages and ducked around a woman stopped on a motorized scooter to reach the main doors.

Inside, he passed through a throng of passengers and those who'd come to see them off or pick them up. He looked around for a screen that showed arriving and departing trains. The station was a noisy place with dozens of people milling about: college students, military men and women on leave, families with small, excited children. There was even a blind man with his seeing-eye dog near the entrance doors handing out some sort of pamphlet.

Freeman pulled a piece of paper with the

information on the train to Kentucky from his pocket and checked the overhead screen. Almost at once he saw that the train had arrived on time…and it was leaving on time. By the big clock on the wall, he had a minute. Maybe less. Heart pounding, he glanced toward the line waiting by the elevators and then walked as quickly as he could manage to the stairs leading to the track level. "Wait for me," he muttered. "Wait for me, Katie." His heart felt as though it was in his throat. Passersby bumped into him, but he paid no heed as he took one step after the next, using the handrail to steady himself.

As he reached the top of the stairs and the open platform, he heard the sound of the wheels on the track. The train was moving out of the station, slowly gathering speed. *"Ne!"* Frantically, he looked along the nearly empty platform. No one sitting on the benches, no familiar Amish dress, no young women at all.

One car after another rolled past. Inside, passengers stared out the windows or settled luggage overhead or under their seat. Freeman scanned the faces. There were no prayer *kapps*. No Katie looking back at him.

He stood there stunned, unmoving, unable to accept his loss as the train pulled away. *"Ach*, Katie," he rasped. He leaned against the wall. "What have we done to each other?" Her merry face rose in his mind's eye. He could almost hear the peal of her laughter, see the way she tilted her head when she giggled.

A uniformed Amtrak employee pushed a broom down the platform, cleaning up dust and litter. He leaned down to pick up a candy bar wrapper. "Can I help you, sir?" he asked.

Freeman shook his head. He glanced around. The two of them appeared to be the only ones left on the platform.

"Are you waiting for the next train?" the young man asked.

Freeman shook his head, but he registered what the young man had said. *The next train.* This wouldn't be the only train. And missing Katie here didn't mean he couldn't catch up with her farther down the line. He'd find the ticket office and buy a ticket on the next train going south. Better yet, he'd have Jerry drive him on to the Philadelphia airport. If he took a plane, he could get to Louisville ahead of Katie.

He started for the stairs.

"There's an elevator there, sir," the boy called after him.

Freeman hesitated. He could manage the stairs again, but the elevator might be faster. He turned back and his heart skipped a beat. Sitting on a black suitcase just beyond the elevator, half-hidden, was a figure in a black dress and bonnet. The woman's face was buried in her hands.

It took a moment for it to register what he was seeing. Whom he was seeing.

"Katie?" he called. Goosebumps rose on his arms. "Katie!" he bellowed.

She looked up, saw him and leaped to her feet. Then she just stood there and stared at him. "Freeman?"

One moment they were both standing on the train platform looking at each other, and the next she was in his arms and he was covering her tear-stained face with kisses. "Oh, Katie, darling," he murmured in Deitsch. "You're here. I found you. I thought I'd lost you. I thought—"

"I couldn't go." Her words came in a rush. "I realized that if I couldn't have you, I wouldn't marry Uriah. It wouldn't be fair to him. I wouldn't marry at all. I couldn't. Loving you, I couldn't, Freeman. I could never love anyone but you. I'm so sorry."

He pulled Katie hard against him and held her, oblivious to the amused gaze of the young Amtrak employee. "Forgive me," he said. "I was wrong. I'm such a fool to quarrel with you over—"

"*Ne*, it was me," Katie insisted, looking up at him, teary-eyed. "I'm the one who—"

"Shh." He kissed her tenderly on the lips.

"Hush, darling, hush," he said. "Just tell me that you'll give me another chance. Give *us* another chance. Marry me, Katie, and I promise I'll never mention Susan again."

"*Ya*, Freeman, I will marry you," she whispered. "And talk about her as much as you want." She gave a little laugh, clinging to him as the sound of an approaching train shook the platform under their feet. "We'll talk about her every day as long as I can be your wife."

"She was right, you know," Freeman said, holding her tightly. "She and I were never meant to be together. I was meant to be *your* husband and none other. Can you forgive a hardheaded—"

"Miller?" Katie finished for him. "The sweetest man…"

The grinding wheels of the approaching train drowned her words, but Freeman stood there, not willing to let her out of his arms, paying no heed to the shriek of brakes and the hiss of the opening doors.

"I love you, Katie Byler," he murmured into her ear. "I always will."

"And I love you," she answered.

"Kiss her again!" the Amtrak employee with the broom urged.

Freeman did just that to the laughter and applause of the arriving passengers.

## Epilogue

Katie laughed as bells on the horse's harness jingled and red and blue lights flashed on Thomas's buggy as he drove over the dam and turned into Freeman's lane. Freeman squeezed her hand in the darkness and her pulse quickened. She was so full of happiness that she thought it must be bubbling out of her and overflowing, filling the buggy and spilling out into the yard.

She wanted to pinch herself to make certain that she wasn't dreaming, that this was her wedding day, and that Freeman, sitting beside her in the buggy, was her husband for now and forever, so long as they both lived. The day had been glorious, everything that every Amish bride hoped for: friends, loved ones, good food, fellowship, God's word and the blessings of church and community. She had so much to be thankful for.

She glanced out at the falling snow. Propane lights shone from the house windows, softened by the swirl of white. This was a gentle snow, billowing flakes spinning through the cold November night to frost everything in a glory of pristine icing.

"We're here!" Thomas proclaimed as he jumped down out of the driver's seat and stomped around to the back of the buggy to open the rear door.

"How deep is it?" Freeman asked.

"Three or four inches." Thomas gazed out into the snow-blanketed barnyard. "But the weatherman forecasted another three before morning."

"Sara says five more inches at least," Ellie chimed in from the front seat where she'd ridden beside Thomas. "I think she's right. It smells like more snow to me."

"It can snow all it likes," Katie said. Ivy and Uncle Jehu were both staying with friends for the next couple of days, and Katie welcomed the thought of being snowed in with Freeman. How wonderful it would be to have a few days shut away from the world together.

Katie looked out the window. The mill loomed big and black in the distance. Not a single star or hint of moonlight pierced the darkness. The only sound was the crunch of snow under Thomas's boots, the creak of the horse's harness and the snort of the horse.

Freeman climbed out and reached to steady her as she prepared to get down. "Careful," he said to her. "The step is slippery." And then to Thomas, he said, "Thanks for getting us here safely."

"Easy enough," his friend replied. "No traffic on the road tonight. A few inches of snow is nothing to a good horse and buggy. By morning, Amish farmers will be pulling Englishers' cars and trucks out of ditches. Those who don't have the sense to wait for the snowplows."

Ellie leaned over the seat back to speak to Thomas. "Still, the sooner we're back to Sara's, the better. You've still got to drive home after you drop me off."

"Got the basket with the food and wedding cake?" Thomas asked.

"*Ya,*" Ellie answered. "Right there." She pointed to a spot on the floor behind the bench seat. "Plenty to keep Katie from cooking for a few days."

"No need to get your shoes wet," Freeman said, looking up at Katie. "Put your arm around my neck."

Katie did and he swept her into his strong arms.

"Careful of your leg!" she warned.

"My leg is fine," he assured her as he carried her to the back porch and set her gently on the step. "Thanks," he said to Thomas. He pushed open the porch door and Katie walked in ahead of him.

"Blessings!" Thomas handed Freeman the basket and headed for the buggy.

"Be happy!" Ellie cried, waving.

Katie smiled and waved back, thinking how fortunate she was to have made such a good friend as Ellie.

"Let's get you inside." Freeman turned the kitchen doorknob and then stepped back to let her cross the threshold ahead of him. "I guess if we were Englishers, I'd be carrying you all the way in."

She laughed. The warm kitchen, so familiar and yet so strange, enveloped her. This is our home, she thought as she walked in, mine and Freeman's. *Our woodstove, our gleaming wooden table with the bouquet of holly leaves and berries, our calendar on the wall.* With trembling fingers, she untied her bonnet strings and slipped off the formal black head covering and her heavy black cape.

Freeman took them from her and hung them on hooks beside his own coat and black wool hat.

"Welcome home, wife," he said huskily. He

set the basket of wedding food in the center of the table.

She swallowed, her own words caught in her throat.

"Happy?" he asked.

She nodded, for once at a loss for words. She was just so filled with joy right now; there weren't words for it.

Freeman took her hand in his warm one and held it. "It's been a long journey getting to this point," he said. "I nearly overturned the apple cart, but I'll try to do better in the future."

"It was no more your fault than mine," she managed, gazing up at his handsome face. "My willfulness. Always wanting to do things my way. I've a lot to learn about marriage."

"Don't we both?" He chuckled. "But we have time and the grace of God to try and get it right." He leaned down and kissed her, a slow, gentle kiss, his lips fitting perfectly to hers, sending sweet sensations of joy radiating through her heart and body. "I love you, Katie Kemp," he said.

"And I love you, Freeman Kemp." She laughed, liking the sound of her new name, and he laughed with her.

"I've a gift for you, darling. Would you like to see it?"

She looked up at him quizzically; it wasn't

their tradition for a man and woman to give each other a gift on their wedding day.

"Yes or no?" he teased.

"Of course!"

Taking Katie's hand, he led her through the kitchen and up the staircase. She'd never been further than the linen closet on the second floor of the farmhouse. She knew this was where the bedroom was that they would share as man and wife, but she had never thought it proper that she go there before they were married.

A propane lamp on a Victorian marble-top table lit the wide upstairs hallway. Wide floorboards of yellow pine stretched the length of the passage. Someone had left an arrangement of pine and holly on the deep windowsill. Katie inhaled the crisp scent of fresh-cut greens.

"Close your eyes," Freeman said as they reached a closed door.

"Should I trust you?" she teased, but did as he asked.

A door hinge squeaked. "Sorry, I'll have to fix that," he said. "All right, you can open your eyes."

It took a moment for Katie to realize what she was looking at and slowly a smile spread across her face. "Did you buy this?" She took in the beautiful pine bed with bluebirds and sheaves of wheat carved into the head and footboard. A tall wardrobe and dresser completed the set.

*"Ne,"* he answered softly. "I made it. The bed. The other pieces were my great grandmother's. I always liked them and I thought you might."

"I do."

"I made the bed just for you, Katie. For no other woman but you." He sounded almost bashful.

She sighed. "I love it, Freeman. I do." She looked up at him through teary eyes. "I'll try to be the best wife to you. I promise."

"And I promise never to expect you to be anyone but yourself."

She smiled at him as she began to remove, one by one, the hairpins that held her starched white prayer *kapp* in place. "And I'll promise to *try* not to be too bossy," she whispered. And then she was in his arms and nothing mattered but the new life that they were beginning together, a life blessed by God and shining with hope.

* * * * *

Dear Reader,

Welcome! I'm always happy to meet new readers and to welcome old friends for a story of romance and faith in the traditional Amish community of Seven Poplars. Once again professional matchmaker Sara Yoder has her task cut out for her with a particularly difficult case. Will independent and outspoken Katie Byler be the girl she can't find a husband for?

Among the Amish, everyone expects to marry and start a new family in the faith. But sensible Katie can't seem to find a beau. She's watched all her friends wed, and now that her brother's brought home a new wife, Katie is desperate enough to consider a match with a Kentucky stranger.

But wily Sarah has another plan. She sends Katie to the home of a prosperous miller, a cantankerous bachelor recovering from a recent accident and an old heartbreak. Freeman needs a temporary housekeeper, a biddable woman who will cook and clean without questioning his authority. Sparks fly when two strong personalities clash. Do opposites attract, or has Sara made her biggest mistake yet?

I hope you'll read this story to find out.

Wishing you peace and joy,

*Emma Miller*

# LARGER-PRINT BOOKS!

## GET 2 FREE
## LARGER-PRINT NOVELS
## PLUS 2 FREE
## MYSTERY GIFTS

*Love Inspired®*
# SUSPENSE
### RIVETING INSPIRATIONAL ROMANCE

## Larger-print novels are now available...

# REQUEST YOUR FREE BOOKS!
## 2 FREE WHOLESOME ROMANCE NOVELS
## IN LARGER PRINT
## PLUS 2
## FREE
## MYSTERY GIFTS

## HEARTWARMING™

### *Wholesome, tender romances*

---

**YES!** Please send me 2 FREE Harlequin® Heartwarming Larger-Print novels and my 2 FREE mystery gifts (gifts worth about $10). After receiving them, if I don't wish to receive any more books, I can return the shipping statement marked "cancel." If I don't cancel, I will receive 4 brand-new larger-print novels every month and be billed just $5.24 per book in the U.S. or $5.99 per book in Canada. That's a savings of at least 19% off the cover price. It's quite a bargain! Shipping and handling is just 50¢ per book in the U.S. and 75¢ per book in Canada.* I understand that accepting the 2 free books and gifts places me under no obligation to buy anything. I can always return a shipment and cancel at any time. Even if I never buy another book, the two free books and gifts are mine to keep forever.

161/361 IDN GHX2

| | |
|---|---|
| Name | (PLEASE PRINT) |

| | |
|---|---|
| Address | Apt. # |

| | | |
|---|---|---|
| City | State/Prov. | Zip/Postal Code |

Signature (if under 18, a parent or guardian must sign)

### Mail to the **Reader Service:**
**IN U.S.A.:** P.O. Box 1867, Buffalo, NY 14240-1867
**IN CANADA:** P.O. Box 609, Fort Erie, Ontario L2A 5X3

\* Terms and prices subject to change without notice. Prices do not include applicable taxes. Sales tax applicable in N.Y. Canadian residents will be charged applicable taxes. Offer not valid in Quebec. This offer is limited to one order per household. Not valid for current subscribers to Harlequin Heartwarming larger-print books. All orders subject to credit approval. Credit or debit balances in a customer's account(s) may be offset by any other outstanding balance owed by or to the customer. Please allow 4 to 6 weeks for delivery. Offer available while quantities last.

---

**Your Privacy**—The Reader Service is committed to protecting your privacy. Our Privacy Policy is available online at www.ReaderService.com or upon request from the Reader Service.

We make a portion of our mailing list available to reputable third parties that offer products we believe may interest you. If you prefer that we not exchange your name with third parties, or if you wish to clarify or modify your communication preferences, please visit us at www.ReaderService.com/consumerchoice or write to us at Reader Service Preference Service, P.O. Box 9062, Buffalo, NY 14240-9062. Include your complete name and address.

HW15

# WESTERN WP PROMISES

**YES!** Please send me **The Western Promises Collection** in Larger Print. This collection begins with 3 FREE books and 2 FREE gifts (gifts valued at approx. $14.00 retail) in the first shipment, along with the other first 4 books from the collection! If I do not cancel, I will receive 8 monthly shipments until I have the entire 51-book Western Promises collection. I will receive 2 or 3 FREE books in each shipment and I will pay just $4.99 US/ $5.89 CDN for each of the other four books in each shipment, plus $2.99 for shipping and handling per shipment. *If I decide to keep the entire collection, I'll have paid for only 32 books, because 19 books are FREE! I understand that accepting the 3 free books and gifts places me under no obligation to buy anything. I can always return a shipment and cancel at any time. My free books and gifts are mine to keep no matter what I decide.

272 HCN 3070 472 HCN 3070

| Name | (PLEASE PRINT) | |
| --- | --- | --- |
| Address | | Apt. # |
| City | State/Prov. | Zip/Postal Code |

Signature (if under 18, a parent or guardian must sign)

### Mail to the **Reader Service:**

**IN U.S.A.:** P.O. Box 1867, Buffalo, NY 14240-1867
**IN CANADA:** P.O. Box 609, Fort Erie, Ontario L2A 5X3

WPBPA16R